~ Sweet Surprises ~

~ Dedication ~

For Eliza

*May you have many true friendships
and lots of sweet surprises*

"Blessed are the pure in heart,
for they will see God."

~ Matthew 5:8 ~

~ A Note From Brianne ~

Hi! My name is Brianne Carmichael, and the True Friendship series is about me and my closest friends. If you have read the Heaven in my Heart series, you know me pretty well by now; but if you haven't had the chance to read about my years as a middle school girl, then I want to give you a quick view of my life up to this point and introduce you to my friends as we begin high school together.

As I said, I'm Brianne, and I am fourteen years old. I live in a small town in Oregon called Clatskanie with my parents and my four younger siblings: J.T., Jeffrey, Steven, and Beth. My dad is a pastor at Rivergate, a community church we've been attending since we moved here during my fifth-grade year, and several of my friends go there too.

Two of my close friends who don't live in Clatskanie with me are Sarah and Joel. Sarah became my best friend when I moved here, but she moved away at the beginning of our seventh grade year. We keep in touch through letters, email, phone calls, and seeing each other whenever we can get together. Sarah is still my best friend even if she lives far away. Joel is one of my best friends too. I knew him before I moved here, and I still see him whenever I go to camp in the summer because he lives there with his family. His parents and mine are close friends too, so sometimes we visit them.

My other best friend is Austin Lockhart. We became friends in seventh grade after Sarah moved away, and we've stayed close ever since. I love his family and spend a lot of time at their house when I can. Some people think Austin and I are dating, but we're not. We spend a lot of time together because we're best friends, and that's what best friends do, right? I've decided I don't want to have a boyfriend right now, not until I'm at least sixteen.

Some of my other friends are Brooke, Marissa, Emily, Allie, and Ashlee. Ashlee and I have our dramatic moments and we're not exactly close, but I care about her and try to be the best friend to her I can be. Another friend I've had some trouble with is Emily, but I'm doing the best I can with our relationship. Emily has always been homeschooled until this year, so going to public high school is a big change for her, but I'm praying it turns out all right and she can have lots to smile about during her freshman year at Clatskanie High.

One other thing you need to know about me is I love Jesus with all my heart. If you don't know much about Him, I hope you will learn a lot by how I live my life and what He teaches me. I try to keep my heart open to God always, and He never stops filling it with lots of good things and sweet surprises. I hope you can experience the same.

~ CHAPTER ONE ~

Dear Sarah,

I finally have my own email address!!! I am so excited! Now I can write to you whenever I want instead of only when I have something really urgent I need to tell you. And you can write me and know it will only be read by me, not my parents or J.T. My mom and dad are still saying no to a cell phone and some other things, but at least this is progress. I'm starting to feel like a responsible teenager instead of a little kid.

I know...I have the best parents and the most perfect family ever. Spare me the lecture. I think I need those things and they would make my life sooo much better, but I don't. I get it. I'm just frustrated sometimes when I see my friends having all these things my mom and dad say I don't need. But as Austin says, he can have them now and doesn't want them, not even email, so I suppose I can be satisfied too.

Enough about that. How was your first day? Do you have any classes with any of your friends? Did you meet anyone new? Today didn't feel much different for me than last year since we're still in the same building and just using different classrooms, but it feels cool to be in high school. I have two classes with Austin, two with Marissa, one with Allie, and one with Emily, but none with Brooke. That's a bummer. Emily is in choir with me, and we sat together today. She has at least one person she knows in each of her classes, so that's a big answer to prayer. I hope you can make some great friends this year, Sarah. In fact, I'm really praying for it! So let me know how your first day went :)

Love you,
Brianne

P.S. He is my God and I am trusting Him!!!

Sarah smiled and let out a sigh. She was glad Brianne had good news to share. Brianne was her best friend in the world, and Sarah always wanted things to be good for her. In fact, she had prayed for that more than anything since leaving her hometown of Clatskanie two years ago.

But the last two years had been difficult for herself. More than she had ever imagined. Friendships had been hard to come by—first at her middle school in Portland, and then here in Eugene when her family moved again during her eighth-grade year.

It wasn't that she didn't have any friends. She did. Most of her classmates liked her fine, and she didn't feel like she had any blatant enemies. And today had been okay in terms of seeing some of those friends in her classes, having lunch with Hannah, Kaelyn, and Chelsey—three girls she also went to church with, and going to volleyball practice this afternoon, but she didn't have that one special friend like Brianne. Someone she could be completely herself with and talk to about everything.

She was glad Brianne had an email address now. They had been writing letters to each other ever since she had moved away, but having to wait a week or more to hear back from her best friend had been difficult at times. Being able to share about a tough day, or to share good news and hear back from Brianne the same day would be nice—more like if they were still living in the same town and saw each other every day.

Hitting the reply button and typing out her news, she tried to keep it simple and honest. She didn't make it sound better than it had been, but she didn't focus on the negative either. Overall it had been an okay day. Nothing spectacular, but it could have been worse. Much worse, actually, so she was thankful.

She also had an email from Ryan, and she read his message and responded to his similar questions. Ryan lived in Portland and had attended the same middle school and church with her there. They had been boyfriend and girlfriend for a few months but had broken up when she began to feel they were spending too much time together and ignoring their other friendships.

They hadn't really dated, just spent some time together outside of school. They'd never kissed, but Ryan had been a special friend. After their breakup, near the end of seventh grade, he hadn't spoken to her for several weeks, and that had been difficult, but over the summer they went back to being friends and remained so until she moved. Since then he'd written to her two or three times a week, and she always enjoyed hearing from him and sharing her thoughts. If there was anyone she would consider to be a close friend besides Brianne, it was Ryan; but she often held back in telling him everything on her heart, not wanting to become too attached to another friend who was so far away.

So she kept it light and simple with him. Honest, but nothing too deep. Closing her laptop and going downstairs, she helped her mom with setting the table and felt ready for dinner. She was used to eating breakfast and lunch and having snacks whenever she was hungry instead of having to eat according to her school schedule, and she realized she hadn't had anything to eat since noon.

Having dinner with her family was typical. Her mom and dad were both there, along with her older brother, Scott. He was starting college in a few weeks, but he was living here and commuting for his first year, and she was glad. Having him away would be hard on her.

If there was one good thing about her family moving twice in two years, they had stayed close. That had been especially true since moving here. Her dad had the job he wanted, and her mom didn't have to work anymore. She'd spent more time with her family than hanging out with friends, and she knew a lot of other kids couldn't say that. Some of them didn't want to say that, but others wished their parents were home more or had close relationships with their siblings, and she had both.

Her mom had already asked about her day on the drive home from volleyball practice, but her dad asked now, and she shared the same things she had told her mom, Brianne, and Ryan.

"When is your first game?" he asked.

"Next week, on Thursday. It's a non-league practice match, but it's here. Can you come? The freshmen play at four."

"Yeah, I might be able to do that," her dad said. He had a flexible schedule most afternoons now.

"I'll be there," Scott said. "I don't have to work on Thursdays."

"Awesome!" she said. "How about you, Mom? Will my whole family actually be there to see me play for once?"

"Yes, I believe so," she replied. "That's a nice switch from last year, huh?"

"Yeah, definitely," she laughed. "From the last *two* years. None of you have seen me play since sixth grade!"

"Are you any better?" Scott teased her.

"I hope so."

They all laughed, and her blah day suddenly seemed better. She had homework to do after dinner, but not much. The math was review for her, and she had to read the first few chapters of a novel her English teacher had handed out today. Neither of those were especially difficult, just took time, but she was finished by seven-thirty.

She went downstairs to see what Scott was doing. He had worked the early shift today at the restaurant where he was a dishwasher and bus-boy, and he didn't have a girlfriend, so he'd been home all evening. She found him in the family room looking over the college course schedule. He had decided what classes to take this fall, but he needed to pick the specific days and times.

"Am I interrupting?" she asked.

"Nope," he replied, highlighting one of the classes with the pen in his hand. "What's up, Sare Bear?"

She smiled. He used to call her that a lot. "Sare Bear? I'm in high school now not preschool."

"You'll always be Sare Bear to me."

"I finished my homework and thought I'd come see what my brother is up to."

"Not much," he said. "No homework for me yet, and there's nothing on TV. Nothing worth watching anyway."

She leaned against him, and he lifted his arm to put it around her shoulders. Being with her brother always gave her a safe and loved feeling.

"How was today, really?" he asked.

"Okay."

"Anything bad happen?"

"No."

"Anything good? I mean really good?"

"Brianne has her own email."

"I'm not talking about Brianne. I'm talking about school."

"Then, no. Not really. It wasn't bad, just not great."

"Describe a perfect day. What do you wish would have happened?"

She laughed. "Found out Brianne is moving here."

"Besides that. Something realistic."

She thought about it for a moment and then came to a hopeful conclusion. "Well, it might have happened. I may have met my new best friend today, I just don't know it yet."

~ CHAPTER TWO ~

Sarah's second day of school was about the same as the first. The main difference she noticed between middle school and high school was how much older the juniors and seniors seemed. Yesterday had been for freshmen only, but with the school filled to capacity and walking among seventeen and eighteen year olds, she felt very young in comparison.

She was used to being around older high school students at church, but there was something different about sharing hallways and other common areas with them here. For the most part she felt ignored by them, even the guys, but they were difficult for her to ignore. The girls were overdramatic about everything, and the guys were tall, even huge in some cases.

She knew not all of the upperclassmen fit one of those categories. There were plenty of ordinary, average students who didn't command attention, but there were enough to make her feel like she had entered a whole new world.

When school let out at 2:10, she had volleyball practice in the gym, and she headed there like she had yesterday. One of the girls she'd been getting to know over the last couple of weeks while they were having tryouts caught up with her as she was about to enter the locker room.

"Hi, Sarah," she said.

"Hi, Annalise," she replied. "How was your day?"

"Okay. How about you?"

"Fine."

"What classes did you have?"

"Home Ec, Computers, and French," she said.

Their high school was on a block schedule. They had four of their classes on Mondays and Wednesdays, and the other four on Tuesdays and Thursdays. Fridays rotated from week to week. Yesterday she'd had Algebra, Honors English, Earth Science, and P.E. Today she'd had her other three classes plus study period.

"When do you have study period?" Annalise asked.

"Second," she replied. "I'm sure it will be nice in the future, but it made this morning drag."

"I had it last today, so I had some things to do. The teachers are piling on the homework already."

"I had some yesterday but not today," Sarah said.

"That's nice."

"Yeah, especially since I have youth group tonight."

"Me too," Annalise said. "What church do you go to?"

"Divine Love Fellowship."

"Oh, I wish I could go there. Everyone goes there."

They did have a large youth group, and Sarah liked it. "Like who?" she asked, wondering whom Annalise was friends with.

Annalise was changing into her shorts and t-shirt. She'd had on a really cute skirt and top Sarah had noticed but hadn't had a chance to say anything about.

Annalise said a bunch of names as she was undressing and redressing. Sarah knew most of them by name but not super well as friends, except for Hannah and Kaelyn.

"You know Hannah and Kaelyn?"

"We went to Meadow View together."

Hannah and Kaelyn were best friends, like she and Brianne were. They had accepted her as one of their friends, and apparently Annalise too, but up until now she had only seen them at church.

She'd had math with them yesterday, Kaelyn was in her Home Economics class, and they had lunch together yesterday and today, but she didn't feel like she could have a friendship with them that could match what they had with each other.

"Would your mom and dad let you come to youth group at Divine Love if someone invited you?"

"Maybe," she said. "We go to a really small church, and there aren't any girls my age."

"If you want to come sometime, you could come with me."

Annalise smiled. "That would be so cool! I'll have to ask, but could I come tonight?"

Sarah laughed. "Sure, if you want to. Let me know."

***

Brianne sat down beside Austin on the bus, feeling tired from the long day. After spending her summer doing a variety of things—going to different places, having a lot of time with her closest friends, and being on vacation with her family, being at school all day yesterday and today had wiped her out. The excitement of the first day had worn off, and today reminded her how much teachers loved to give homework. It had been a good day but tiring.

"Did your class run the mile today?" Austin asked. He knew she had just come from P.E. He had it first thing in the morning, and she had it at the end of the day.

"Yes."

"What was your time?"

"Slow," she laughed. "But I wasn't last."

"Who's in your class?"

"Nobody except Jason and a few other guys I know. No girls I hang out with."

"Are you making any new friends?"

She thought about that. She had talked with some girls yesterday and today she knew but didn't have close relationships with, but she wasn't opposed to changing that.

"Not so far, but it's only the second day. How about you?"

"I have a new guy in my P.E. class, and he's in band too. He plays the trumpet."

"Did he just move here?"

"Yes. Over the summer."

"What's his name?"

"Tyler. They moved from Astoria. He hates it."

She laughed. "Why?"

"He likes the coast."

She could see that. "Why did they move?"

"His dad's job."

"Where does he live?"

"On Hazel Grove Road."

"That's close to Emily."

"Yep. How did she seem today?"

"About the same. I didn't talk to her much because we started working on a song in choir today."

"Are you regretting taking choir instead of band?"

"I don't know yet. I think I'm going to miss it, but I like being able to just sing."

***

On Wednesday afternoon, Emily Hawthorne rode home on the school bus for the first time in her life. After being homeschooled since preschool, she had begun attending Clatskanie High yesterday, and she wasn't thrilled about it.

Yesterday her mom drove her to school and picked her up, along with her two younger sisters. She had gotten the time off work for the momentous day, but today she only took them on her way to the doctor's office where she worked as a nurse. She didn't get off until five, and her dad was on the road—delivering a freight-load of something to Seattle. He would be back tomorrow, but for today she and her sisters were on their own for the next couple of hours.

On a typical Wednesday, she would have done her studies at home in the morning and early afternoon. Right about now she would be heading to ballet class or a music lesson, but instead she was riding this stinky bus, hearing all kinds of conversation and horrible language being used, and she didn't understand how her life could have taken this horrible turn.

She had never considered going to public school. She had no desire and no reason to believe she would ever have to. Sometimes her parents had talked about sending her to a private high school when she got to be this age, and she might have been okay with that, but when her dad's work hours were cut in half, that option had flown out the window along with homeschooling. She had tried to convince her parents she could study on her own at home while her mom was at work, but they didn't think she was ready for it. Maybe for her junior and senior year, but not now.

Her friend Brooke was sitting beside her, seeming oblivious to the craziness around them, and Brooke's stop was near the beginning of the route, so she would be alone soon. Allie rode this bus too and lived on her street, but she was on the soccer team and they had practices and games after school this time of year, so she wouldn't be riding the long stretch with her until November. One of her sisters was in sixth grade. The middle school students got out at the same time, but Elise had a good friend from church she was sitting with, and her youngest sister was only in fourth grade.

The elementary school got out an hour later, and Erin would ride home alone, something Emily did not like at all. Erin was very shy around new people, and she cried yesterday when her mom took her to school. Emily hadn't heard the report from this morning, but she had visions of Erin crying all day at school and on the bus ride home as she sat all alone in a sea of strange kids who might do or say who-knows-what to her.

It all seemed so unfair and wrong. Her friends had been trying to tell her it would be okay, but they didn't understand. They couldn't relate. It was fine for them because they were used to it, and public school was all they'd ever known. But she wasn't used to it and didn't see herself ever getting there.

~ CHAPTER THREE ~

Brooke Quan said good-bye to Emily. Rising to follow other students who lived in her neighborhood, she walked down the aisle and stepped off the school bus. Her house wasn't far, and she walked the short route by herself. Her sister was a senior this year, but Brenda had cheerleading practice after school every day.

She didn't have much homework tonight but enough to get started after making a small snack. Her mom had restocked the refrigerator yesterday, and she had been craving a strawberry smoothie since the beginning of her last class. She liked her schedule though. She did her best thinking in the morning when she had math, science, and Spanish, along with band. In the afternoon she had literature, P.E., and study period.

The only bummer was not having any classes with her two closest friends, Brianne and Emily. But she did have one less-close friend in each of her classes. Band and science with Austin; Geometry with Caitlin; Spanish and P.E. with Marissa; Literature with Allie; and study period with Lindsay.

Lindsay was her newest friend. They met last year in P.E. and ran together on running days. Lindsay was really sweet and quiet like herself, but when they were together they talked nonstop.

She wished she had at least one class with Emily and Brianne, but for different reasons. She wanted to help Emily with her adjustment to public school, but seeing Brianne had more to do with their friendship. Brianne was her best friend ever, and she was always happy when they were together.

They got along really well, had a lot of fun, and could talk about anything. She was glad they would see each other at church twice a week, but at church she had to share her with everyone else.

She wanted to call Brianne like she had yesterday, but she decided to get her homework done first, hoping Brianne would call her this time because it would make her feel like Brianne missed her too instead of it being one-sided. She honestly didn't believe that, but sometimes she wondered what she had to offer her. Brianne had so many friends, and she was her quietest one.

The phone rang before she got her binder and math book out of her backpack. Seeing it was Brianne made her smile.

"How was your day?" Brianne asked.

"Good. I like my classes and schedule."

"Me too," Brianne said. "Except for P.E. and not having any classes with you."

"And only two with Austin?"

"Yes, but at least we have two and ride the same bus. I really do miss you, Brooke. We're going to have to make a habit of spending time together after school, like every Tuesday or something. Would that work for you?"

"Yeah. You could come home with me."

"Would another day be better?"

"Tuesdays are good, or Thursday if you want to stay for dinner and go to youth group together."

"That might work, then I wouldn't have to get a ride home."

"Do you want to plan on it for this week?"

"Yes!" Brianne laughed. "Ohh, that makes my day."

They talked for a long time. Yesterday had been informative about their schedules and how the first day of school had been for each of them, but today they talked about the things they usually did, which included Brianne sharing her insecurities, concerns, and hopes with her.

"How did Emily seem today?" Brianne asked.

"She was quiet on the bus. I asked how her day was, and she said, 'Awful', but she didn't say why."

"You know who I think she has the most classes with?"

"Who?"

"Ashlee Moore."

"Really?"

"I looked at Emily's schedule yesterday and again today at lunch. I had just seen Ashlee's schedule in math during third period, and I know they have P.E. together because they have it with Austin too, and I'm pretty sure they have literature second, French fourth, and cooking seventh."

"Wow, that's harsh."

"I know. That would be hard on me, and we've been getting along well lately."

"I haven't seen Ashlee except for today at lunch when we saw her in line."

"I have math with her, but she didn't sit by us yesterday or today."

"Why haven't they gotten along? Emily's never said anything about it."

"I don't know for sure. Some things happened before I ever moved here. Austin thinks it has something to do with their families, but he doesn't know the story either. I don't think anyone does except Ashlee and Emily."

"Strange. Maybe she'll tell me one of these days."

"Whatever it is, I wish they could both let it go. I can see being mad at people for awhile, but to hold a grudge for years and years? I don't see how that helps anything. If I held on to all the things Ashlee has said and done to me, I would be a miserable person. I'd rather let it go, move on, and be happy."

***

When Brianne got done talking to Brooke, she decided to call Emily. She waited a few minutes in case Brooke had in mind to do the same. She knew Emily would probably rather hear from Brooke than her, but Brooke sounded like she was going to do her homework, and if Emily was home alone with her two sisters, she knew a quick phone call would probably be a welcome thing, even if it was her.

Brianne didn't know why Emily didn't want to embrace her friendship, and she didn't want to force it on her, feeling content to let Brooke, Allie, and others be there for her as much as Emily would allow them to be.

But she did want to let her know she was thinking about her, she cared, and she was still here if she ever needed to talk or whatever.

Many times she felt like giving up altogether, feeling that would be best for Emily, but God had continued to place a concern for Emily on her heart and say, 'Hang in there, Brianne. One of these days she's going to need you, and I know you'll want to be there for her.'

So for today she made the call, and when Emily answered, she did her best to sound casual but concerned. Not overly so but enough to let Emily know she was one of her friends and cared enough to check on her.

Emily didn't talk much, mostly giving one-word answers to her questions. She didn't sound distracted, like she had other things to do, just distant and noncommittal—typical of how their conversations went on the phone or face to face.

"I guess I should get some homework done," she finally said. "Bye, Emily. See you tomorrow."

"Okay, bye," she replied.

Brianne hung up and a usual depression began to overtake her, but before she could sink too low, the phone rang and she answered it. Hearing Austin's voice made her mood brighten.

They had seen each other on the bus this afternoon, but he forgot to ask her something. "I was thinking since we have study period together and we can work in pairs as long as we don't get too crazy, do you want to bring some of David's songs tomorrow? You have some ready to show me, right?"

"Yeah, I could do that."

"Cool. I think I'd rather do that than homework if I can get away with it."

"Unless you need my help with math?" she teased him.

"Oh, that's right. We have math first. I'll see how much I get tomorrow."

One of the things she liked most about her friendship with Austin was they helped each other. She helped him with math, he helped her with science. She encouraged him in his musical talents, and he helped her with understanding people she didn't understand.

"Was it you who's been on the phone the past half-hour or someone else?"

"Me," she replied. "I called Brooke first and then Emily."

"How did that go?"

"About how I expected."

"I'm going to get her together with Tyler."

"Who's Tyler—oh, that new guy?"

"Yeah, the one from Astoria. They can be down on life together."

"What's he like, besides upset about moving?"

"He's nice. I talked to him today about coming to youth group tomorrow, but he's joining marching band and they have practice on Thursday nights."

"Is he cute?"

"How am I supposed to know, and why do you care? You have David."

She laughed. "I'm not wondering for me."

"He's not a redhead, but I think Emily would say he's pretty good-looking. You know, like me."

"That cute, huh? Maybe I will have to check him out."

"Okay, I need to call all my other girlfriends now."

"Have you noticed any new girls?" she asked seriously, recalling a few new faces.

"I haven't noticed," he said. "I'm not on the look-out for anyone."

He said it too seriously for her to tease him this time, and his sincerity reminded her of what a good friend he was. Someone she could always count on.

"You know what the best part of my day was?"

"What?"

"You," she replied. "It's official. We're ninth graders now and you're still my best friend."

"You didn't forget about me while I was in Montana, huh?"

"Nope. I just missed you."

"I missed you too. We haven't had a movie night in awhile. How about Friday?"

"Okay. It's a date."

~ CHAPTER FOUR ~

Brianne got some interesting news from her mom and dad that night before she went to bed. They had all gone to church this evening for the midweek children's program her three youngest siblings participated in. She and her twelve year old brother, J.T., helped out, and her mom was one of the teachers. Her dad often had meetings or met with people for counseling during that time, but she knew he had a meeting with the church board members tonight that seemed to be out of the ordinary, something that usually made her nervous. One of her greatest fears was they would have to move again, either because the church decided it was time to look for a new pastor or because her dad decided it was time to move on to a new church.

He didn't say anything on the way home, but Brianne had the feeling he had something to tell them. After her mom had gotten Beth, Steven, and Jeffrey into bed, she and J.T. were summoned to the kitchen for a mini family meeting.

"We have some good news we want to tell you," her dad said, making her feel less nervous this had anything to do with them moving. "It's not for sure yet, because there's a few more things to finalize, but it looks like the

35

church is going to be giving me a raise at the beginning of November. I requested it awhile back because this house is really small and the bigger you kids get, the smaller it gets, so we'd like to find a bigger place."

"Really?" Brianne asked, feeling absolutely giddy at the prospect.

"Yep," her dad replied.

"Cool!" J.T. said. "Does that mean I get my own room?"

"Maybe. We would like to get at least one more bedroom than we have here. How do you feel about still sharing a room with Beth, Brianne?"

Brianne hadn't allowed herself to imagine moving to a different house here in Clatskanie. Sometimes she had imagined having her own room like she used to before Beth had joined their family, but she didn't have to think about it for too long before saying what she knew was true.

"I don't mind sharing with Beth. I'm used to it, and I know she is. I'd rather have a bigger living room or a basement than my own room."

"We're not telling the other kids until it's official, but we wanted to tell both of you, and you can let some of your friends know so if there's something on their street for rent, we can check it out."

"Okay," Brianne said, thinking immediately of Brooke and if there might be something in her neighborhood they could afford. The houses were all new and large with nice yards, and it would be wonderful to live so close to Brooke.

In the morning she told Austin the news, but he already knew. His dad was on the budget committee and had known about it for several weeks.

"And you didn't tell me?"

"I wasn't supposed to," he said. "I'm glad you finally know. That was not an easy secret to keep from you."

"I'm so excited!" she said. "I'm so ready to be out of that tiny house."

"And have your own room?"

"I'll probably still share with Beth unless we can find a house with five bedrooms and she wants her own, but it would be nice to have a bigger space to share."

"When are you going to start looking?"

"I'm not sure, but my parents said we could tell our friends and ask if anyone knows of places for rent. I'm going to ask Brooke for sure. I love the houses in her neighborhood."

"They're nice," Austin said.

"I know, and Josh and Anna live there too along with Pastor Nate and Janie. That would be really cool! Oh, by the way, I'm going over to Brooke's house after school today, so I won't be on the bus."

"Three days into school and you're already abandoning me?"

She laughed and knew he would be fine without her this afternoon, but his words did make her wonder what it would be like to live further away from Austin and not be on the same bus with him anymore. She knew she would still see him a lot, but he was always a welcome sight first thing in the morning, and they usually talked nonstop on the afternoon ride. He was the first person who knew if she'd had a bad day, and he always made it end well.

They received an assignment in math that morning, but the teacher gave them time in class to work on it, so during study period Brianne showed Austin a few of David's songs that were her favorites of the ones he had sent her after meeting him at camp. He had a lot, and she liked most of them, but these had stood out to her for one reason or another. Her favorite was titled *Sweet Surprises.*

"How about you?" she asked after Austin had taken the stack from her and put it into his notebook to look over more later at home. "Have you written any new songs you want to share with me?"

"I was thinking we could work on one together."

"How come?" she asked.

"Because I think it would be fun?" he replied.

She smiled. "Yes, it would be. Maybe on Friday. We could hike up to the ridge. I always think the best thoughts about God when I'm outside."

He was looking at her, and there was something unique about that moment. Sitting there in the middle of a classroom where others were all around and yet they were having a private conversation: it reminded her of several moments they'd had together this summer.

"I'm looking forward to singing with you at youth group tonight," he said. "We haven't since camp."

"I know. It's hard to believe that was almost a month ago. What are we singing?"

Normally they had rehearsal for the upcoming week, but a lot of people were gone over the holiday weekend, so they hadn't gotten together and Austin had volunteered to lead. He wasn't sure if they would have a full band tonight. Emily was the only one who said she would be there for sure. He had several songs in mind, including *Let It Shine*.

After school she went home with Brooke, and they walked around her neighborhood to see if there were any houses for rent. They saw one, but it looked small. There were a few larger ones for sale, but she knew her parents weren't looking to buy. With her dad being a pastor, they needed the freedom to pack up and move quickly if God led them to another church, something she didn't like the thought of having to do, but she knew it was a reality she might face.

"It would be awesome if you could live in this neighborhood," Brooke said. "But are you sure you want to move this far away from Austin?"

"I'll still see him every day," she said like it wasn't a big deal, but in her heart she knew it might be, and she wasn't sure her dad would want to be so far from the church. It wasn't that far, and plenty of people who lived on this side of town attended there, but it was more than the two-minute drive they had now.

"What did he say when you told him?"

Brianne remembered Austin's words about her abandoning him, but she told Brooke what he told her first. "He already knew and is excited for us."

"Are you guys going to the football game tomorrow?"

"Me and Austin?"

"Yes."

"No. Why?"

"I just thought maybe you were."

Brianne didn't always tell her other friends when she had special plans with Austin. Not because she was trying to hide it, but just because she didn't want them to make spending time with him something it wasn't. Brianne knew Brooke was going to the game with her family because they always went to support her sister as one of the cheerleaders.

"Are you going to the dance?" Brianne asked, knowing there was one afterwards because they had been promoting it all week at school.

"By myself? No thanks."

Brianne didn't comment on her words for now, but she wondered if Austin might like to go to the dance with her and Brooke so Brooke could go without having to go alone. She hadn't gone to dances in seventh or eighth grade because she wasn't interested, and she wasn't now either, but if Brooke wanted to go, she would be willing to go with her, even if it meant giving up her movie night with Austin.

They left for youth group after dinner, and Brianne was happy to be back after being in Washington with her family for the last two weeks. Austin had been able to practice with Marissa for a half-hour before everyone began arriving, so they both played guitar together, Emily played keyboard, and Brianne sang with them. Next week they were hoping to have a full band, but Brianne thought it sounded fine.

When they went to sit down, Austin whispered he would be back in a minute and continued walking past the rows of chairs toward Pastor Nate's office, a large kitchen, some classrooms, and the restrooms. She assumed he was going to the bathroom and expected him to return in a minute or two, but when he didn't she began to wonder where he'd gone.

She waited ten minutes and then decided to check and see if he was okay. She glanced at the office window on her way past, but it was dark in there. The kitchen was also empty, and none of the classroom doors were open or had light coming through the windows. She was about to assume he must be in the bathroom where she couldn't go check on him, of course, and hoping he wasn't sick, but then she noticed the outside door at the end of the hall was open a bit.

It was usually closed and locked from the outside, but if he had gone out there he wouldn't close it completely so he could get back in. Pushing it open fully and stepping outside, she whispered his name and asked if he was out here. There was a light above the door, but her eyes weren't adjusted enough to see him if he was.

"I'm here," he replied.

She looked in the direction of his voice and could barely make out his silhouette along the walkway. Closing the door carefully so it remained unlocked, she stepped toward him and asked why he was out here.

"Just thinking," he said.

"About what?"

He remained evasive. "Stuff."

She went from being curious to concerned. "Is something wrong?"

He looked at her but didn't say anything. She stepped closer until she was right beside him.

"Feel like sharing with your best friend?"

"Tonight was hard for me," he said.

She was surprised. From her perspective it had gone really well, and he'd seemed relaxed about it.

"Why was it hard?"

"I'm fourteen, Brianne. What am I doing leading juniors and seniors?"

"You did at camp."

"Not on my own. Justin was the leader, and I didn't know the kids there. If some of these guys had been there that week, I would have felt how I did tonight."

She wondered if he was mad at her for talking him into leading on a regular basis, but she didn't regret it from the standpoint of how much she enjoyed singing with him, nor how well it had sounded from her perspective. She gave him a hug and said what she knew he needed to hear.

"You were great. It sounded good. Don't let anyone look down on you because you're only fourteen."

He didn't say anything. She stepped back and smiled.

"Besides, you'll be fifteen in another month."

He didn't seem encouraged by that. He may be turning fifteen, but he was still a freshman.

"Are you mad at me for talking you into this?"

"No."

"Do you want to go back to playing drums? You can. It's not like we've made some big announcement you're the new worship leader."

"That's what I'm out here trying to figure out: if I should be doing this, and if I want to."

"What does God say?"

"Crazy stuff."

She laughed. "So what you're really thinking about is if you're going to listen?"

"Yeah, I guess."

Brianne got a new view of Austin then. She already knew the fun-loving side and had been experiencing his genuine friendship for a couple of years. And she'd certainly seen him as a Jesus-follower with special gifts, but tonight he seemed scared of it. Humbled and broken before God.

"Do you want me to leave you to that then?" she asked, feeling prepared to go back inside if he needed private time with God more than he needed her words of advice and encouragement.

"No, I was about to go in."

They walked to the door, and he opened it. She stepped ahead of him, and once they were inside, he said something else. "Thanks for coming to check on me."

She was about to respond, but he interrupted.

"I know. That's what friends are for."

She smiled. She did often tell him that, but she was actually going to say something else. "Whenever you need to talk, I'm here."

~ CHAPTER FIVE ~

On Friday Brianne entered the choir room and took her seat beside Emily. She was having a good day, but she was glad it was the end of the week. She was looking forward to spending the afternoon and evening with Austin, sleeping-in tomorrow, and having a lazy Saturday. During study period she had talked to Austin about possibly going to the football game tonight and the dance afterwards with Brooke and some of their other friends who were going, but he didn't want to. He said it was fine if she wanted to go with Brooke instead of having movie-night with him, but she didn't want to choose the game and dance over that. Maybe another Friday she would go if Brooke wanted to, but not tonight. She needed extended time with her best friend, and she didn't want to cancel on Austin. Even if he said it was fine, she knew he would be disappointed, and she would be too.

She talked to Emily for a minute before class got started. Emily said she'd had an 'okay' week but didn't elaborate much on what she'd liked and hadn't. Emily did say choir was her favorite class so far, and Brianne was enjoying it too. She liked all of her classes for different reasons. Some because of the class itself, and others because of whom she had the class with. Thus far she was enjoying choir for the singing aspect more than because of Emily, but she was glad they had one class together and hoped with time they could be closer friends. She wanted Emily to receive her friendship as much as she wanted to give it.

Their choir teacher, Mrs. O'Conner, had them do warm-up exercises, and then she had an announcement to make before they would begin working on the song she had passed out.

"The fall play this year is going to be a musical. Mr. Watkins, the drama teacher, is looking for cast members who can sing as well as act, and there are quite a few parts that require both talents. If you're interested in trying out, I have practice scripts here you can take after class, and auditions will be held next Wednesday and Thursday after school."

Brianne turned to Emily and spoke without hesitation. "You should try out."

"Yeah, maybe," Emily said without a lot of enthusiasm, but it was the most positive she had heard Emily be about anything this week.

Brianne didn't think about trying out herself until after class when she steered Emily toward the practice scripts and Mrs. O'Conner met them there, asking if they were interested.

"Emily is," she said, not caring if Emily thought she was being too pushy. She knew Emily wanted to.

"Great!" their teacher said. "How about you, Brianne?"

"I don't think so. I haven't had much experience with acting," she said, feeling like her small part in the seventh-grade winter play and a few roles she'd done for church didn't qualify her for being in an all-school production in high school. Maybe in two or three years when she was an upperclassman, but not as a ninth-grader.

"This might be your chance to get some experience," Mrs. O'Conner said, handing her a practice script along with passing one to Emily.

Brianne didn't want to be rude, so she took the papers and supposed there were enough packets or Mrs. O'Conner wouldn't be so quick to give her one. Walking beside Emily as they exited the room, she was more focused on getting Emily to try out, and she said something she believed to be true.

"You could get a part so easy, Em. I know it."

"I'll look over it," she said. "I don't want anything with too many lines. I'm better at singing and dancing than acting."

Brianne decided not to say anything else. Emily didn't have a lot of self-esteem in interacting with her peers on a normal day-to-day basis, but when it came to performing and doing things she was good at, she generally had confidence in herself and her abilities. If being in the school play was something she wanted to do, she likely would, and if she didn't want to, Brianne didn't want to force her into it.

Emily didn't say anything to her about trying out as well, and Brianne wasn't looking for her to, but after school when she mentioned the play to Austin and how she had encouraged Emily to think about it, his response echoed her choir teacher's words.

"What about you?"

"What about me?"

"You're going to try out too, aren't you?"

"I don't think so."

"Why not?"

She shrugged. "I'm not a strong singer, and I haven't done much acting. I'm sure there are a lot more talented people at this school than me."

"Do you want to?" he pressed. "I mean, if you got a part, do you think you'd like it?"

"I guess." She had always enjoyed being in plays in the past. "But this is a high school play, not—"

"And we're in high school now. Who do you think they fill these parts with? College students?"

She laughed. "No, but I doubt many freshmen will get speaking roles. I think Emily has a good shot at it, but me? Not likely."

"I'll try out if you will," he said.

Brianne didn't know why she hadn't thought about Austin wanting to try out. He had the acting and singing talent, but she hadn't imagined him being interested.

"You will?"

"Sure. I'm not a football player. I can't be in marching band because they practice on Thursday nights. I've gotta get the girls' attention somehow."

She laughed. At the end of the summer she'd learned Austin had started learning to play drums and guitar to impress Sarah when they were in sixth grade.

"Have you met any new girls this week?" she asked him again, honestly curious.

"No."

"Do you wish we went to a high school where we would be meeting a lot of new kids?"

He shrugged. "Not really. Do you?"

"I don't know. Meeting a lot of new people can be good, but challenging too."

"Have you heard from Sarah?"

"Yes, every day this week."

"And she's doing okay?"

"Yeah. Nothing too dramatic. She likes high school better than middle school so far, and she likes her volleyball teammates."

"How about Joel? Have you heard from him since camp?"

"No. I'll probably write to him soon, but he doesn't have email, so I won't expect an immediate reply. He's usually slow about writing me back, and if he writes to me before I get around to it, I'll be shocked!"

"Would you write to me if I lived far away?"

"Why, are you moving?"

"No, I'm just asking."

"Then no need to discuss it."

He laughed at her adamant refusal to talk about the possibility of them living far away from each other in the future. But she wasn't laughing. She had already lost two close friends to distance, and she didn't want Austin to be added to that list.

***

"Hi, can I sit here?"

Emily looked up and saw a boy standing in the aisle of the bus. He was looking at her. She recognized him because he was in a few of her classes and he was also a friend of Austin's, but she had never spoken to him directly.

"Sure," she said, wondering why he was asking, but as he sat down she realized the bus was mostly full and there weren't many empty seats left. She'd had her nose in a book and hadn't noticed how much time had passed.

The bus began to move after he sat down, and she wondered why he was so late. She had noticed he rode this bus, but he was usually already seated near the middle when she took a seat closer to the front with Brooke. Brooke had ice skating lessons on Friday afternoons right after school, so her mom had picked her up today, leaving her to ride the bus on her own for the first time.

Tyler didn't say anything and neither did she. In addition to having some classes with her, he also had been sitting with Austin and their other friends from church during lunch the last couple days. He was usually quiet, and so was she. Emily didn't mind having a quiet personality, except when she was with someone else who was equally quiet, and then she hated it. She tried to go back to reading her book, but after reading another paragraph, she knew she wasn't concentrating and had missed what was happening in the story.

Too much time had passed for her to ask Tyler why he had been so late, so she thought for a moment but couldn't think of anything else to say. Going back to her reading, she tried harder to concentrate on the story and had begun to get lost in it when the bus made its first stop at the housing development where Brooke lived.

A lot of kids got off there, and she knew seats around them would open up. She hoped Tyler would choose to move. It wasn't that she didn't like him or want to be around him, she just didn't know him well and felt like he was in her personal space. And the not-talking thing made her uncomfortable as well. It magnified how much she hated being around kids she didn't know and being thrust into an environment she didn't want to be in.

But he didn't move to a different seat, and once the bus was moving again, she decided she was going to have to say something. His stop was after hers, which was still fifteen minutes away, and if he sat beside her the whole way, she would go crazy with the silence.

Turning to look at him with something in mind to say, she started to speak but then realized he was listening to something on his iPod. Nixing the idea to attempt a conversation, she began to go back to her book, but he glanced over and caught her looking at him.

"Did you say something?" he asked, pulling one of the earbuds out.

"Oh, no," she replied, feeling flustered. "I was just going to ask you something."

He kept looking at her, and she realized he was waiting for her to go ahead. With him sitting so close, she noticed something about him for the first time. His eyes were green, and they were really nice. She'd never seen such beautiful green eyes before. Now she felt flustered for interrupting his music listening and because of his striking gaze.

"How long have you and Austin been friends?"

He gave her a strange look. "Four days, I guess."

"You weren't friends in middle school?"

"I just moved here two weeks ago. I met him on Tuesday."

"Oh," she said. "I thought you were a friend of his from school."

"What do you mean, 'from school'?"

Now she felt flustered by the color of his eyes and the miscommunication they were having. "Um, I know Austin from church," she said, trying to explain. "So we have a lot of mutual friends, but most of his friends from school I don't know—unless they come with him to church sometimes."

"You just moved here too?" he asked.

"No, I've lived here my whole life—practically anyway."

He continued to look puzzled, and she knew why.

"I was homeschooled before this year. That's why I don't know Austin's school friends. Where did you move from?"

"Astoria," he said. "And I lived there my whole life."

She thought of something for the first time. "I guess I sort of feel like we moved. We still live in the same house, but everything is different."

He didn't say anything, and she didn't know what else to say. "Anyway, you can go back to your music. I was just wondering how long you've known Austin."

"It's not music," he replied. "It's a book."

"What book?"

Once she asked, she felt like she was being nosy, but it was too late to take it back, and she was honestly curious. What did a fourteen year old, public-school boy read?

"20,000 Leagues Under the Sea."

"Really?"

"Yep."

"I love Jules Verne!"

He reached for the book in her hands and folded the front half over so he could see the title. "Much better than a vampire story."

She felt embarrassed. She didn't usually read popular teen fiction stories about vampires or fantasy in general, but one of her friends had given her the book to borrow, insisting she had to read 'the best book ever.' So far she thought it was okay. It was well written and intriguing, but not exactly thought-provoking or valuable in a literary or spiritual nature. Just something to occupy her time for a few hours.

"I agree," she laughed. "Want to trade?"

He smiled. "No, thanks."

He went back to listening, and she went back to her book, but she couldn't get into the story. She put the book away when she got to the end of the chapter and just looked out the window as they passed familiar scenes on the rural road. When they came to another stop, Tyler got her attention by tapping on her shoulder.

She turned and saw him holding out one of the earbuds to her. "Do you want to listen? It's the best part."

She smiled and took the earpiece from him. Inserting it in her ear, she had to listen for a moment to hear where they were, but she agreed it was the best scene. They didn't get all the way through it before they came to her stop, but she had enjoyed being in the world of Jules Verne for a few minutes and felt like she might go home and take the classic-bound book from the shelf in her room and read it cover-to-cover over the weekend. She only had a little bit of homework and no plans except worship-band practice tomorrow afternoon and church on Sunday morning.

"Thanks," she said, handing it back to him and picking up her backpack from the floor between her purple canvas shoes as the bus came to a stop at the end of her driveway.

"Have a nice weekend, Emily."

"Bye," she said. "See you Monday."

~ CHAPTER SIX ~

Sarah left the locker room and walked toward the outside door where someone would be coming to pick her up. She wasn't sure if it would be her mom, dad, or Scott. So far it had been a different member of her family each day. She'd been having a good week at her new school, and volleyball practice was fun.

"Hey, Sarah. Wait up," she heard someone say. Turning around, she saw it was Annalise.

"Oh, I thought you already left," she replied, stopping to wait for her. "Where were you?"

"I had to talk to the coach," she said. "I might have to quit the team."

"Why?"

"My ballet class on Mondays and Thursdays at 6:30 isn't full enough for them to have the second advanced class, so it looks like I'm going to have to join the other one that meets from four to six."

"Did you ask the coach if you can leave early on those days?"

"Yes. She's going to think about it. But a lot of our matches are on Thursdays, so even if she lets me stay on the team, I'll miss half of the games."

"I'm sorry," Sarah said.

"It's okay. I'd rather dance anyway, but this is the first year I've had to choose between them."

They stepped outside, and Sarah saw several cars waiting in the circle, but not one of her family members. It was after four-thirty, so that was unusual, but she supposed someone would be here soon.

"Are you going to the football game tonight?" Annalise asked.

"I don't think so," she replied. She'd heard about the home game during the student assembly at the end of the day, but without her brother on the team as he had been in past years, she didn't see the point.

"If you want to go, my family is. We could pick you up."

Sarah thought that might be fun. She liked Annalise, and doing something with her outside of school and volleyball practice would be a good way to get to know her better, just like on Wednesday when she had come to youth group.

"Okay, maybe," she said. "I'll have to ask. Call me later?"

"Sure," Annalise said, stepping toward the car her mom was driving.

She waved. "Bye."

After Annalise got into the car, she stood there waiting for her ride to come. Several girls on her team and others on JV came out to get into vehicles waiting for them. By 4:45, she knew her family had either forgotten about her or something had delayed whoever had been designated to pick her up. She hoped it wasn't something serious like an accident, and she took out her cell phone. Calling home first, she got no live response. Trying her mom's cell phone, her mom answered.

"Hi, Mom. Is someone coming to get me?"

"Yes. I am. Sorry, honey. The lines at the grocery store were long, and this traffic tonight is crazy. I'm almost there."

"Okay. I was just checking."

She let her mom go and stepped over to a brick-lined flowerbed to sit on the wide ledge and wait. While she was sitting there, one of her volleyball teammates came out with a guy who was obviously her boyfriend. She hadn't seen Britlyn this week except at volleyball practice and during her cooking class she'd only had on Wednesday this week. Britlyn was a really good player and several of the girls had played with her during middle school. They kind of had their own clique going amongst the rest of them on the team, and Sarah hadn't been too impressed with Britlyn or her friends when it came to being nice and having good sportsmanship.

Her mom pulled up about that time, and after she got into the car and her mom drove out of the school parking lot, they passed Britlyn and her boyfriend. They were walking with their arms around each other. Apparently one or both of them lived nearby because they kept walking once they reached the street.

Sarah didn't envy her. She didn't want to think about the kind of relationship they likely had. Normally she tried not to judge others and make assumptions based only on what she could see, but Britlyn wasn't trying to disguise anything by the way she was kissing and hanging all over whatever-his-name and allowing him to have his hands wherever he pleased. Her mom noticed as well.

"Is she on your team?"

"Yes."

She changed the subject. "How was practice?"

"Fine. Annalise might have to quit though, so that's a bummer."

"Is that the girl who went to youth group with you this week?"

"Yes. She invited me to go to the football game with her family tonight. Can I?"

"Sure, if you want."

"I think it would be fun. Annalise is nice, but I don't have much time with her, even during practice."

"Do you have any classes together?"

"No."

"Why might she quit volleyball?"

Sarah explained about her ballet class conflicting with the practice times. Her mom asked if she had made any other new friends this week, and she didn't feel she'd made significant progress to call anyone a new friend yet, but starting high school at the beginning of the year had been better than when she started seventh grade at her middle school in Portland and here halfway through her eighth-grade year.

Annalise called her after dinner, and Sarah said she could go to the game. "Do you want to go to the dance afterwards?" Annalise asked.

Sarah hadn't thought of the possibility, but she went with her first instinct. "No."

"Good. Me neither," Annalise said.

She laughed. "Then why did you ask?"

"I was just talking to Kaelyn, and she and Hannah are going. I thought you might want to go too."

"Not really. I'm not into dancing with guys I don't know, and I don't know many yet."

"Me neither," Anna said. "Well actually, I know a lot of them, but I'd rather not."

They both laughed.

"Just so you know," Sarah said seriously, "I never want you to feel like you have to do something you really don't want to for my sake, Anna. Be honest with me about stuff, okay?"

"Okay. Thanks for saying that. I'm not always good about speaking my mind, especially when it comes to Kaelyn and Hannah. Last year I got into some major trouble when I went along with something I shouldn't have. But it's hard to say no to them sometimes. It's like they don't even give you the option."

"I've noticed that," Sarah replied but didn't want to turn this into a gossip session about their friends. "Well, anyway. I'll see you soon. What time?"

"About 6:45. The game is at 7:00."

***

Brooke tried to call Brianne to see if she had changed her mind about wanting to go to the game tonight, but no one was home. It seemed strange because Brianne hadn't mentioned any family plans at lunch today, but maybe they had decided to go out to dinner or to a movie, or maybe they'd heard about a house for rent they were checking out.

She tried twice. Once right after dinner and again at 6:30, but no one picked up either time. She usually enjoyed going to the football games with her family and watching Brenda cheer, but she felt like going with a friend this time, so she decided to call Emily and see if she was free and wanted to go.

Emily said she did but would have to ask. "Can you hang on a minute, or do you want me to call you back?"

"I'll wait," she said. "We can come pick you up, but we'll have to leave in a few minutes to still make it to the game on time."

Emily put the phone down, and Brooke listened to the silence for a minute before she returned. "I can go," she said. "Does it cost anything?"

"Just a dollar with your ASB card, but we can pay for you. You can bring some money if you want snacks."

"Okay. I'll be ready."

Brooke informed her mom and dad Emily could go, so they hurried to get going and drove the longer distance to pick up Emily and then headed for the high-school stadium. When her family had first moved here before her seventh-grade year, the campus the middle and high school students shared seemed so small compared to those in her hometown in Washington, but she actually liked going to a smaller school now that she was used to it. She didn't feel as lost here, and she had made new friends quickly. Brianne had practically become her best friend on the first day.

She had met Brianne's other friends at school too, and then at the church when she started going to youth group on Thursday nights. That's when she first met

Emily, but they hadn't gotten to be close friends because she only saw her once a week.

But over time she and Emily had gotten more connected, and she considered Emily to be her best friend now besides Brianne. She had been secretly excited when Emily told her the "bad news" about having to go to public school this year, but now she was more bummed about it because she didn't actually have any classes with her. But she still saw her on the bus, during lunch, and at church, and if they could do some things like this together, she would welcome it.

Brianne and Emily were her best friends, but they were complete opposites, and Emily hadn't been receptive to Brianne's friendship lately. Brooke knew it was partly because Emily had a crush on Austin and didn't understand Brianne's close relationship with him. But Brooke knew it also had to do with Brianne's personality and outlook on life being so vastly different than Emily's.

Brianne was friends with everyone. Emily was a loner. Brianne was always happy, even when she had a reason to be unhappy. Emily was down about things a lot, and often when it wasn't that bad. Brianne was a dreamer. Emily was a realist. And her reality was fine, but her view of it wasn't.

One thing they had in common was being the oldest child in their families, but while Brianne embraced it and loved to look after her younger siblings and help them with things, Emily didn't want to be bothered. Brooke knew she loved her sisters and was concerned about them going to public school now too, but she wanted things to be different rather than doing something to help make a difference.

Brianne wasn't especially talented in one particular thing like music, art, or sports; but she sang well, played the flute, ran in track, and enjoyed the things she did even if she wasn't the best at everything. Emily had talent oozing out of her in music, dance, and acting, and she was really smart, but she didn't seem to enjoy those things or like school much—even when she'd been homeschooled. It was like she was great at so many things, but it didn't mean anything to her.

Brooke had learned a lot about herself by having them as friends. She was like Brianne in some ways and Emily in others. Some because she chose to be, and others by default because that was her God-given personality and she couldn't be different no matter how much she wished she was or tried to be.

Mostly she was happy with her life and being who she was, and she was glad both Brianne and Emily accepted her and didn't try to tell her to be different, so she accepted them for who they were too. It was easier with Brianne because she was easy to be around and was a great friend. But she tried to accept Emily for who she was too and be the best friend to her she could be.

They passed through the gate behind her parents and younger brother and searched for seats where they could see Brenda well. The girls were doing pre-game cheers involving acrobatic moves and lifting each other into the air. Brenda was petite and thin, so she was often at the top of the pyramids, standing on another girl's shoulders, or being tossed into the air with her sleek black hair waving in the breeze and her wide smile emerging on her flawless Asian complexion.

If there was one person Brooke was envious of, it was her sister. Brenda was pretty, popular, and practically perfect in every way. She was even nice to her, and they rarely squabbled about things. But Brooke admired her to the point of often feeling inferior and plain in comparison. Brenda had encouraged her to go out for the freshman cheer team this year, but she didn't want to. She didn't have that kind of confidence to be in front of her peers, doing daring stunts, shouting at the top of her lungs, and fitting in with pretty, popular girls like that.

Her current ambition was to continue becoming a better ice skater. She had been taking figure skating lessons for the last four years and putting in extra practice sessions for the last year and a half. She was getting pretty good now. She could do a lot of jumps and spins, and she had placed well in her most recent competition before the summer. She had her first one of this season coming up in two weeks, and she wanted to do well: to be as flawless and graceful and powerful as her sister was as a tiny dynamo of a cheerleader, only all by herself on ice.

~ CHAPTER SEVEN ~

Emily was in awe of Brooke's sister during the cheerleaders' pre-game routines. She had seen those kinds of stunts performed for cheer competitions, and she was always fascinated, but Brenda was simply awesome. She made it look effortless and appeared to be having so much fun. It made her want to try out for the squad next year, but she didn't know if she could make it or have the courage to try.

Once the game started, the cheerleaders did more of what their title implied, leading the crowd in standard cheers rather than performing, and her attention was drawn elsewhere. She didn't know a lot about football, so watching the players set up in formation and run a play didn't interest her much unless someone caught a long pass or one of the players had a big run that got the crowd cheering.

She found herself watching those around her and talking to Brooke more than anything. After the first quarter ended, Brooke suggested going to the snack bar, and she agreed. They each got hot chocolate, a bag of popcorn, and a long red licorice rope. Walking back to the stands, Emily followed Brooke up the steps to where they had been sitting and heard someone call her name just before she reached their row.

Turning toward the sound, she saw a lot of faces, most that weren't looking her way, and those who were she didn't recognize. She had met a lot of new people this week, so it could have been anyone, although she couldn't imagine who would be shouting out her name.

She was about to turn back and continue to her seat, supposing whoever it was had been calling another Emily in the crowd, but she heard it again.

"Emily!"

The sound of the male voice was followed by seeing someone waving his arms out of the corner of her eye. Looking that direction, she realized it was someone in the band, but she didn't recognize him.

"Hey!" he shouted over the crowd beginning to cheer about something, but she didn't turn away to see what was happening on the field. She realized it was Tyler as the crowd between them stood to their feet and blocked her view.

The sound around her became deafening, and she looked out at the field, knowing something major had happened but not certain what it was until the announcer blared, "Touchdown!"

The band began to play the school fight song, and it was pandemonium around her as she finally got to her seat and stood beside Brooke who was cheering along with everyone else. Emily was glad she had been the one to carry the popcorn or it would likely be on the ground by now. In her excitement, Brooke had already splashed a bit of hot chocolate onto her gloved hand she was wiping with a napkin, but she didn't seem to care.

The crowd quieted down for a moment when the band stopped playing, and Emily saw they were kicking for the extra point following the touchdown. She didn't know a lot about football, but she knew that much. She didn't expect the crowd to go wild and the band to start playing again when the ball went sailing through the uprights, but they did, and it was almost as crazy as the first time only didn't last as long.

It wasn't until she was sitting down again she remembered Tyler, and she tried to spot him, but a lot of the band members looked the same in their uniforms, and she couldn't remember where exactly he'd been sitting. She kept scanning and had settled on it being that guy, that one, or that one, until Brooke's voice broke into her intense searching.

"Who are you looking at?"

She wasn't sure what to say. Apparently Brooke hadn't heard Tyler calling her name before the big touchdown or seen him waving his arms to get her attention. Brooke knew Tyler as well as she did, but Emily didn't think he had been calling both of their names.

"I was looking for Tyler. I remembered he's in the band. Do you see him?"

"Austin's new friend, Tyler?"

"Yes."

"Hard to tell from this angle," Brooke said.

"What instrument does he play?"

"Trumpet," Brooke replied. Brooke was in band with Tyler and Austin, but she played the oboe, which wasn't a marching band instrument, and she had youth group on Thursday nights anyway. "Oh, I think that's him!"

"Which one?"

"Third row down, one-two-three-four-five from the left."

Emily scanned to the appropriate spot, and she thought Brooke was right, but she couldn't tell for sure without him turning—

"Hey, Tyler!" Brooke shouted in a loud voice Emily didn't know she possessed. Brooke was usually much more reserved and quiet. Emily turned toward her instead of keeping her eyes on the band, and Brooke waved at the same moment. "It's him!" she added.

Emily turned and saw him looking their direction, waving back at Brooke, and smiling. Emily smiled also, but she didn't stand up and wave like Brooke was doing. Brooke sat down, appearing satisfied with the exchange.

"Sorry, I get a little crazy at these games. I didn't shout in your ear, did I?"

Emily turned her eyes away from Tyler and laughed. "No, but who are you, and what have you done with my quiet friend?"

Brooke laughed. "I can be crazy. I'm not a quiet girl all the time."

"Obviously."

Brooke went back to watching the game and standing up to cheer at the appropriate times, but Emily kept glancing at Tyler and waiting to see if he would turn around and look at her. She hadn't thought about him since getting home, grabbing a snack, and going up to her room to read from the beginning of *20,000 Leagues Under the Sea,* but seeing him again made her recall the conversation they'd had and the way she leaned close to him to listen to the story.

She remembered smelling a faint hint of his shampoo, seeing the color of his eyes, and the way he smiled at her before she stepped past him and said good-bye. She hadn't thought much of it at the time, but recalling it now, she was almost certain it was a different kind of smile than she had seen from him all week.

The band performed at halftime, marching out onto the field and playing a couple of recognizable tunes while they mostly stood in a block formation on either side of the fifty-yard line. Emily supposed they hadn't had much time to practice something more fancy and complicated yet, but even in its simplicity it was the most entertaining part of the night since the pre-game cheer routines, although Brooke's abnormal shout-out was a close second.

After halftime, the band apparently had a break because most of the seats were empty during the third quarter, and the fight song wasn't played when Clatskanie got another touchdown. Emily supposed most of the band members were hanging out by the concession stands, and she was tempted to suggest going to get another snack so they might run into Tyler, but she wasn't bold enough to do it, fearing Brooke would guess her true intentions or they would actually see him and she wouldn't know what to say.

When she saw the band members returning to their seats with two minutes left in the third-quarter, she kept waiting to see Tyler, and she finally did, but he didn't look her way, and she felt herself getting a little depressed about it. She had sudden mood-swings sometimes, and she knew it better than anyone. She couldn't help it. A moment of pure elation was usually followed by disappointment, but she never seemed to remember that until it was happening. She often told herself to not get so happy about stuff, so she wouldn't have as far to plummet into despair, but sometimes she got excited and hopeful about something without realizing until it was too late.

Her week had been better than she'd expected it to be. It hadn't been great, but not awful. The kids at school had been nicer than she was expecting. The teachers seemed competent, appeared comfortable dealing with teenagers, and were neither too lenient nor overbearing. Her French teacher was really sweet and spoke the language like she'd been born there, and her science teacher was really funny. She liked choir a lot too.

But she told herself every day to not let herself believe public high school was going to be okay after all. Even if she had a good day, the next was sure to disappoint, so she had remained skeptical and kept her expectations low. Seeing Tyler waving at her and calling her name had been the first time in a long time she had allowed herself to be hopeful and happy about something, but now he was ignoring her, and why shouldn't he? Why had she thought the bus ride meant anything special to him? Why did she see him shouting out her name in a crowded football stadium as something to smile about? Why had she jumped to stupid conclusions about the way he looked at her, or smiled, or shared his audio book?

The fourth quarter had barely gotten started when the Clatskanie team scored another touchdown. The crowd cheered, the band played, someone above them was throwing confetti that landed in her hair and on her jeans, but she remained seated, feeling unable to participate in the excitement. The band was just a sad reminder of the reality Tyler had already forgotten about her.

"You okay, Em?"

She looked over and saw Brooke sit down beside her. The crowd had gone quiet for the point-after attempt, but most people were still standing, waiting to celebrate again.

"Yeah, fine," she said, knowing she sounded melancholy and depressed. Acting that way seemed to dull the pain.

"You don't look fine," Brooke said.

"Just tired, I guess," she replied.

She didn't want Brooke to feel bad for inviting her, but she wanted to go home and go to bed. Brooke didn't say anything else, and she knew her friend had no idea what to do with her when she was like this. But Brooke usually tried something to cheer her up or get her mind off whatever was bothering her.

"I need to go to the bathroom," Brooke said after a few moments. "Do you want to go with me?"

"Sure," she said.

It wasn't until they were walking down the steps she remembered they would be walking past the band, but she refused to glance over and see if Tyler noticed her walking by. He was on the other end anyway, and she knew he had forgotten about her by now. Her stubbornness made her feel stronger and less defeated, and while they were in the restrooms that smelled weird and were a mess, she came up from the plummet she

71

had taken and was feeling more normal by the time they returned to their seats. She hadn't glanced Tyler's way, and she felt proud of herself, but she didn't allow herself to be happy. Just neutral. Safe. In autopilot mode until she could get home and forget this night had ever existed.

About two minutes later, someone walked toward her she didn't take notice of until the girl wearing a long red scarf, matching sneakers, and red mittens was standing in front of her.

"Are you Emily?" she said.

She looked up and saw her face. It wasn't someone she knew. "Yes."

The girl smiled. "Then this is for you," she said, holding out a folded piece of paper and turning away as soon as Emily took it from her gloved fingers. She didn't have a chance to thank her.

Staring at the white piece of paper contrasting with the deep purple mittens she was wearing, she couldn't move until Brooke said something.

"Who's it from?"

"I don't know."

"Open it!"

Emily felt nothing as she unfolded the note, but when she saw whom it was from, that changed rapidly.

Hi, Emily. Are you going to the dance tonight? I am, and I hope you are too. See you then if you are. −Tyler

~ CHAPTER EIGHT ~

Brooke leaned close to Emily and read the note in her hands. She felt shocked by it, but Emily's behavior when she had been trying to pick out Tyler in the band suddenly made sense. Had something happened between them at school today? Emily hadn't seemed distracted at lunch, the time when they both saw him, but she didn't know if Emily had any classes with him and might have talked to him more this week than she knew about.

"Em!" she laughed. "What haven't you told me?"

"Nothing," Emily said. "Well, besides sitting with him on the bus ride home today."

"You did?"

"It was nothing. He was late getting on the bus, and the spot next to me was one of the few untaken seats. He sat with me, but that's it."

"I don't think Tyler saw it that way. Do you have any classes with him?"

"Yes, but we don't talk. Not until today."

"Whatever you said must have left an impression. Do you want to go?"

"No!" Emily said, sounding horrified at the prospect. But Brooke waited for her to change her tune on that.

Emily could be unpredictable. Brooke didn't know how she would act on any given day or what might set off a good or bad mood.

"I don't!" she insisted.

"Okay, I believe you. But it's kind of sweet, don't you think?"

Emily's expression softened. "Yes. But I can't go to the dance. My parents won't let me."

Brooke knew Emily's parents were strict, so she didn't question it or voice her thought about Emily spending the night at her house and going to the dance without her parents knowing about it. She knew that wouldn't be right and didn't want to tempt Emily to do such a thing, but she had another suggestion.

"You should write him back. Just to let him know you won't be there." She said it more matter-of-factly than like a suggestion. If Emily had to do this on her own, she would likely take the no-response road, but with a little encouragement she might do something.

"I'll take it to him for you," she said further.

"Okay," Emily replied.

"Hurry! The game is almost over."

In reality it wasn't, the last two minutes could drag on forever, but she didn't want Emily thinking too much about this. Asking her mom if she had a pen, she got it and handed the pen over to her friend.

"What do I say?" Emily asked, putting the note on the bench between them so she had a hard surface to write on. There was space at the bottom for her to write something, but not much.

"Just you won't be there and why."

Emily wrote something, but Brooke couldn't read her delicate cursive writing upside-down. When she was finished, she folded the note quickly and handed the paper to her like she wanted to do this before she changed her mind.

Brooke went down the steps to the bottom and then up the next aisle. Spotting Tyler two-thirds of the way up in the band, she waved to get his attention, and he looked at her expectantly. She held up the note, and he came into the aisle to take it from her. By the look on her face, he guessed it was bad news.

"She's not going?"

"No, sorry."

He opened the note and read it. Brooke supposed her mission was finished and was about to turn away, but Tyler's smile stopped her, and she waited to see if he would disclose Emily's message.

"Why didn't she give me this herself?" he asked.

"Emily is shy. I think she was shocked."

"Shy?" he said. "She was really talkative on the bus today."

"Was she?"

"Tell her it's okay," he said. "Maybe some other time."

"You should sit near us on the bus," she suggested.

The crowd started to cheer, and they both realized something good was happening on the field. She turned to look and saw one of their players sprinting into the end zone. She cheered along with the crowd and heard the band start to play the fight song. Tyler had gone to his seat, and she went back to hers as well.

"What did he say?" Emily asked over the noise of the crowd.

"He understands. I think he's disappointed though," she said, knowing she could say that based on the look on his face. "What did you say in the note? He smiled when he read it."

Emily smiled also.

"What did you say!"

"Nothing," she laughed. "Just that I would dance with him if I could go, but I can't."

Brooke smiled. "You like him."

Emily didn't deny it and had a faint look of dreamy hope cross her face, something Brooke had never seen from her before. "Maybe," she replied. "I don't exactly know him."

"I think he's interested in getting to know you. How does that make you feel?"

"Hopeful, I guess. Maybe you're right about there being other guys in this world besides Austin."

***

Brianne had a carefree feeling. She and Austin had been up on the ridge, working on a song together for the last two hours. It had been a lot of fun, and now they were heading down the hill with plans to watch a movie.

She thought about where her other friends were tonight, and she prayed for each one silently. Austin was being quiet, and she was lost in her thoughts until they reached the house. Stepping inside, she took off her shoes by the door and walked to the family room in her pink socks. Mariah and Eliza were there. Mariah was

Austin's younger sister, and Eliza was her best friend. They were both in sixth grade this year.

Mariah had become clingy with her over the summer, but she hadn't seen her for about a month except briefly at church on Thursday night. Brianne was excited to have her in the youth group this year, and she had told her so this week. Mariah and Eliza hadn't been here earlier because they had Girl Scouts on Fridays after school and then Eliza's mom had picked them up and taken them both to Eliza's house for dinner. But she had been expecting them to be here now because Eliza was spending the night.

"Hey, you two," she said. "You're here!"

"Hi, Brianne," Mariah said, coming over to give her a hug.

Eliza was shy and didn't do the same, but Brianne said hello to her and asked what they were doing.

"We were playing Wii, but Mom said we have to get out of here now and let you and Austin have your movie date."

Brianne smiled. "No need to rush away. We're going to have ice cream first. Do you want some?"

"Sure," Mariah said.

She went into the kitchen with them, and for the next fifteen minutes the three of them dished up their dessert, sat at the table to eat, and talked about school and stuff. Austin was mostly silent, letting her have time with his sister and her friend and chat about things he didn't have much to comment on. When he was finished with his ice cream, he took his bowl to the sink and then disappeared for several minutes.

Brianne didn't see him again until after she had used the bathroom and returned to the family room. Mrs. Lockhart had come into the kitchen to shoo Mariah and Eliza off to Mariah's room where they could stay up for awhile before they needed to turn out the lights and go to sleep, and she had followed them down the hall to say good-night to them there.

Brianne sat down on the couch. Austin put the movie in and came to sit beside her. He forwarded it to the DVD menu and asked if she was ready to watch.

"Sure," she said.

"Are you glad you're here?"

"Absolutely," she replied.

"It's not too late, we could go to the dance."

"No, this is better."

He smiled and started the movie. It was one neither of them had seen. She'd heard from Sarah it was good and really funny, and she was looking forward to enjoying the story and funny moments with her best friend. She liked so many things about Austin, but one of them was they could laugh together.

About halfway through the movie, the phone rang and his dad answered it. He came into the family room to tell Austin it was for him. She didn't mind the interruption, and it was actually good because her sides were starting to hurt from laughing so much. Austin was gone for a minute or two. When he returned, he had an interesting look on his face.

"Who was that?" she asked.

"Tyler."

Brianne had seen Tyler at lunch on Thursday and Friday this week when he came to sit with Austin, and he was in her literature class, although she hadn't realized who he was until then. She hadn't talked to him much. Even though she had lunch with Austin, she tended to talk more with Brooke, Emily and other girls who joined them, and let Austin talk more with his guy friends. They all sat at the same table together, but the guys were on one end and the girls were on the other. She had study period with Austin right after lunch, so if she had something she wanted to tell him, she usually waited until then.

All she knew about Tyler was what Austin had told her, which wasn't a lot. He had just moved here from Astoria, he wasn't happy about it, and he lived somewhere near Emily, but she didn't remember that until Austin spoke.

"He was calling to ask me for Emily's phone number."

Brianne felt her eyes grow large. "Why?"

"He sat with her on the bus ride home today, and then saw her again at the game. I guess he wants to talk to her more."

"At the football game?"

"Yes. Tyler is in the band, and Emily was there."

"Did you give him her number?"

"No, I said he was going to have to ask her. We have it, but it's unlisted, even in the church directory, so I know her parents are selective about who they give it out to."

"Do you think that's a good thing?" she asked. "Him wanting to call her?"

"Not sure," he replied.

"Does he go to church anywhere? Do you know?"

"I don't think so. We haven't discussed it, but whenever I've mentioned church stuff, he hasn't said anything about his family looking for a church or being a Christian too."

Brianne's hopes deflated a bit. She knew Emily having a guy pay special attention to her would be a welcome change and could help Emily with accepting her fate of having to attend public school this year. She had told Emily maybe God had a sweet surprise waiting for her, and she really hoped that was true: for Emily's sake so she would have something to smile about, and because she was always telling her to trust God and expect great things from Him.

But if Tyler didn't know God and Emily did like him, that could be disastrous. Emily could decide to rebel against her parents' rules about whom she spent time with, or she could be submissive to them and God's warning about becoming too emotionally involved with a boy who didn't share her faith, but be miserable about it.

Austin had a more optimistic view and shared it with her before she could voice her concerned one.

"You know what I said to Tyler this morning?"

"What?"

"I asked him if he was getting used to being here yet, and he said meeting me was the only good thing so far. So I said I would pray for something way better than that. Just kind of joking, and he laughed, but maybe God was listening."

Brianne smiled but still felt cautious. "But if—"

"We'll let God take care of it, okay? I'll pray for Tyler, and you pray for Emily, and we'll see how He answers."

Brianne's heart felt lighter about Emily, but she also felt something concerning Austin. He had always been more mature than most guys his age, but he was maturing right before her eyes, spiritually especially. His faith was becoming more and more real for him, and she didn't want to squelch that in any way, even with her own negative outlook.

"Okay," she said. "We'll do that."

~ CHAPTER NINE ~

On Saturday morning, Brianne and her family went to see two houses for rent. The first place was large and had everything they would need and more, but it was far outside of town and would be a long drive to the church for her dad, and a long bus ride to school. Her mom and dad told the owners they would think about it, but once they were all back in the van, her dad said he didn't think it was going to work for them because of the distance, and Brianne agreed. It wasn't close to any of her friends, and she knew that was an important factor for her. She would rather remain where they were and have a small house than move out here.

The second place was better in terms of location, had four bedrooms, a living room and a family room, and it also had an attic loft that could be her bedroom if she wanted to turn it into one. They liked the house itself, and Brianne knew it had plenty of space on the inside, but it had almost no yard and was really close to the street.

After living in the country with five acres surrounding them, it seemed odd to have no place to go outside except a little patio area in the back and from the front door to the street. It seemed promising while they were there, but after they got home and discussed the two places as a family, everyone agreed having no yard space was a big deal for them, especially her brothers. Whenever the weather allowed, they were outside more than they were inside.

Her mom and dad said they would keep looking, and Brianne realized finding another house might be more difficult than she thought. But she also realized their house, although small, had a lot of positive features. Going for a walk down the driveway to get the mail that afternoon, she was reminded of the open space here and how much she loved it. Walking from the house to the mailbox took two full minutes.

There was mail in the box, but nothing for her. On the walk back she looked at the surrounding landscape, the open fields of wild grass and tall fir trees, and it was beautiful. Clean air. A light breeze. Wispy clouds overhead and the sound of gravel crunching under her feet. It was hard to believe they had lived here for almost four years, and it had become home to her as much as any place ever had.

Why is it when I finally get something I've wanted for a long time, I realize I don't want it as much as I thought? Why haven't I seen all of this beauty before? Why have I been thinking I have it so bad when I don't? Why do I always want things to be different than they already are?

Feeling thoughtful and not having anything to do right now, she sat on the porch steps to pet Belle and think about what she wished was different in her life. A lot of things came to mind, but as she thought each one through, she knew none of it was terrible. Yes, Sarah lived far away, but Austin and Brooke were right here and she had seen them every day this week. No, she didn't have any classes with Brooke, but they got along really well and Brianne knew they were there for each other. Yes, she had friends who were a pain sometimes, and school and youth group had their challenges, but at least she had lived here long enough to develop some complicated relationships, and she had seen a lot of great things happen.

She almost went inside and wrote an email to Sarah with her thoughts fresh in her mind, but she decided to call Austin. He let her talk without interrupting, and then he said something funny to lighten the moment and make her laugh.

"Why weren't you having all these thoughts yesterday when we were trying to write a song? This is way better than the stuff we came up with."

"Sorry, I'm a little behind when it comes to being inspired," she laughed. "Speaking of music, are we having band practice later?"

"Yes. I was calling people before you interrupted. It's at 4:30. We can pick you up."

"Okay. Are you leading?"

"Yes. It will be Pastor Nate and me this week; Marissa and Nate next week; And Marissa and me the following week."

"You must have talked to Pastor Nate since last night."

"Yes. He called me this morning, and we had a good talk."

"I'm glad."

"You know what he said?"

"What?"

"The same thing you did."

She smiled.

"I told him that too, and you know what he said?"

"What?"

"Listen to her. What are you talking to me for?"

She laughed.

"Pray for me, okay? I know you're right. I know Nate's right. But I need more than what I know, you know?"

"Yes, I know. Me too. I have plenty of my own issues. It's taken me four years to realize I live in a great place! And now that I actually appreciate it, we're moving!"

He laughed. "Jesus will provide another great place, Brianne. Your family does need more space."

"You know what I'm hoping for most?"

"What?"

"That it's not too far from here."

"You mean too far from me?"

"Yes, that's what I mean."

"I knew you were going to look at that place today out in the boonies because my dad told me about it, and I was like, 'Please God, no.'"

"Lucky for you, my dad doesn't want to be far from the church."

"That's good to hear."

She talked to him until it was time for them to come pick her up. Band practice went really well. Austin seemed back to his happy, confident self, and Pastor Nate took them all out for pizza afterwards. His wife, Janie, came to meet them, and Brianne liked being out with the smaller group that included her close friends and few older high schoolers Pastor Nate had talked to about being a part of the worship team.

Emily was there, and she seemed to be in good spirits. Austin didn't say anything to her about Tyler calling him last night, and Brianne didn't either. She didn't even say anything about her going to the game because she would have no way of knowing that if it hadn't been for Tyler's call.

Pastor Nate offered to give them a ride home after the others left. On the way, Austin asked her if she wanted to come to his house, and she said that was fine. It was cooler than yesterday, so they spent most of the evening in his room, working on the song they had started yesterday—throwing out the generic lines and replacing them with her thoughts from today and the words Austin had taken to heart.

Spending so much time hanging out with him in his room had a different feel to it than other times she'd been here. The door was open, so they weren't where others couldn't plainly see what they were doing, but being in his personal space for an extended amount of time, writing a song together, and hanging out like the best friends they were: it gave her a unique feeling. Being away from him for the past month and then having this week with him, last night, and tonight: it was nice to know they were picking up from where they'd been during their week at camp together.

They were watching funny videos online when his dad came to see if she was ready to go. It was the time she told her parents she would be home. Austin had one more video he wanted to look at and told his dad so. "We'll be there in a minute."

His dad disappeared again, and they watched the last one of cute tricks this guy had taught his dog and cat to do together. She was in hysterics by the time it finished, and she had to make herself stop so she could breathe.

"Too funny," Austin said, logging off the website and rising from the chair. "Time to go, Cinderella. Your pumpkin carriage awaits."

"This was fun," she said, meaning that seriously. "Thanks for having me over."

"Anytime," he said. "You can invite yourself whenever you want."

Beth was awake when she got home, and she read to her before she turned out the light. Going to the living room with stationery to write a letter to Sarah, she sat on the couch and the words flowed easily from her thoughts to her pen.

Dear Sarah,

Hi! I've been enjoying our emails this week, but tonight I'm in the mood to write you a long letter. One where I don't tell you the details of my day but look back on the week and share how I'm feeling. I had a good week. How about you?

It was good to see Austin every day. I didn't miss him too much when we were in Washington and while he was still in Montana, but now that I can see him all the time again, I'm really glad. We had movie-night at his house last night, and I was back over there this evening just hanging out, but there isn't anything I'd rather do with my time—except have a visit from you, of course.

I think Emily had an okay week. I encouraged her to try out for the fall play, and she might. I also sat by her in choir and at lunch, but I tried not to be too 'See, high school is great!' I'll let her be the judge of that herself, and I hope it turns out to be a positive experience for her, but that has to happen on her terms, not mine. (A wise friend told me that.) There's a new guy at school Austin has become friends with who might have a crush on her. I don't know him well enough to say if that would be a good thing or not, but I wonder how she would handle it if he does. I feel the need to pray for her on it, so I'll ask you to pray too.

We went to look at a couple of houses today, but neither were what we're looking for. They were both nice in certain ways, but I'm realizing it may take awhile to find the right house for us. In the meantime, God is helping me to see all the great things about being here for the last four years, not the least of which was having you for a neighbor. And after looking at places in different parts of town, I'm hoping we can find something close to where we are now. Riding the bus with

Austin is my favorite time of the day, and I don't want to give that up.

Even as she wrote the words, she wondered if that was something she might have to do. She knew if God led their family to another area of town, He would have His reasons, but she asked Him for what she wanted.

Don't separate me from another one of my best friends, even by a few miles! In fact, forget it, Jesus. I don't want to move. Just keep us here. I'll never complain about this house again. Forgive me for ever wanting anything else.

She was satisfied to leave it at that, but Jesus had some words of His own for her.

Oh, Brianne. Just trust Me. I've already got it all worked out. No worries. I'll give you what you need and more. I promise.

~ CHAPTER TEN ~

On Sunday morning Emily made the trip to church with her family. They had to be there early, as usual, because her mom played the piano for the service at eleven o'clock and had rehearsal with the worship team at 8:30.

Her mom also led the singing for the primary grades and taught the second and third graders during their class time. Her dad taught one of the adult classes, and he had copies to make and other things to get ready, so she was in charge of keeping her nine year old sister, Erin, entertained for thirty minutes until her teacher would be here. Elise was content with reading a book during the waiting time, as she herself would be, but Erin wasn't much of a reader, so the only way to keep her pacified for that long was to read to her, which Emily did every Sunday morning.

She didn't mind the reading part, it was all the times Erin interrupted with questions that made it tiresome. Whenever something was going on in a story she didn't understand, Erin would have her explain it. Whenever there was a word she didn't know the meaning of, Emily would have to give a synonym to help her learn it, to which Erin would always say, 'Then why don't they just say _____?' And whenever a character did something Erin thought was dumb, she would go into this big long explanation of what she would do if it was her.

Her mother said Erin had a good mind for storytelling and would probably end up being a famous writer someday. She could already write good stories on her own when she was in the mood, but Emily saw her as being pesky. Earlier in the week she had been concerned for Erin about having to go to public school, but after the first couple of days, she had adjusted quickly and came home on Friday afternoon announcing, 'Going to school is so much better than being home all day.'

Emily inwardly groaned and hoped she wouldn't repeat the words to her parents at dinner that night, but she did. Erin had been her greatest hope for her parents deciding public school wasn't going to work for their family and would figure out a way to go back to the way things had been before, but her biggest ally in the fight was now her greatest foe.

Emily always read to Erin in the church lobby because there was a couch off to the side where they could sit comfortably, and also because when Erin's teacher arrived, she always came in that way, and Erin would latch on to her immediately and follow her upstairs to the children's classrooms. Emily welcomed the moment when Miss Sam arrived, and once they disappeared up the stairs, Emily picked up her book bag, stuck Erin's reading material inside, and walked to the youth building where she could warm up on the keyboard. Some were already there, and seeing Austin, Brianne, Pastor Nathan, Marissa, and other band members getting set up on stage wasn't surprising, but there was a face among the small crowd she was surprised to see, although he didn't appear the least bit surprised to see her.

"Hi, Emily," Tyler said, noticing her first because he was practically right inside the doorway, shooting baskets at the back of the room free of any chairs and generally used for such activity.

"Tyler!" she said, not hiding her surprise but feeling surprised at her friendly greeting. She didn't usually greet anyone that way, let alone some guy at her school she had talked to for the first time two days ago.

He smiled. "Surprised to see me?" he said, walking toward her with the basketball in his hands.

"Yes! What are you doing here?"

"I came with Austin," he said.

Emily wasn't surprised by that, she supposed. Austin often invited his school friends to church, and since Tyler was new, maybe his family was looking for someplace to attend.

"He said you would be here," Tyler added, and she didn't miss the tone in his voice that implied she was one of the reasons he had come.

"Why would he say that?" she asked, feeling surprised she could speak. He was close enough for her to see his green eyes looking at her, and there was a steadiness to his gaze that made her feel self-conscious and strange. She wasn't used to guys being so focused on her.

"I called him and asked for your phone number, but he wouldn't give it to me because he wasn't sure you would want me to know. So he invited me to come here today and talk to you face to face."

She had no idea what to say. This was so unexpected, there wasn't a word for it. This wasn't the way her life worked. Everything was always planned and predictable. Controlled. She was always in control, or safe in her parents' control over her life, but this was so random and astounding and...inconceivable!

"You're here," she said, smiling at him sweetly and letting her mild embarrassment show. He was making her uncomfortable, and he seemed to know it, but that made her comfortable somehow.

"I know you need to get up there," he said, glancing at the stage. "But maybe afterwards we can talk more."

"Okay," she said. "I'm glad you're here."

"Me too," he replied.

She stepped away and walked toward the stage, turning back to smile at him over her shoulder, and he was just standing there watching her. After she looked away, she heard him bounce the basketball, and he was shooting hoops by the time she reached the keyboard and stepped behind it to turn it on and make sure it was plugged in and ready to go.

She tried not to look at anyone when she stepped onto the stage, which wasn't unusual. Normally she remained in her own world and only interacted with others when they initiated it. But today she knew her friends were looking for a reaction from her concerning Tyler's unexpected presence.

Once she had her music out and warmed up her fingers sufficiently, she glanced up to scan the room and see where Tyler was now. She hadn't heard the basketball bouncing on the floor for a few minutes, and his absence from that area was confirmed easily, but it didn't take her long to spot him. Pastor Nathan had gone to chat with him, and she watched them talking for a few seconds but looked away before Tyler or anyone else could catch her doing so.

But her wandering eyes made contact with Brianne next, and the look on her face was unmistakable. Brianne knew something was going on, and she was curious about it, but she had the giddy look on her face Emily felt in her heart, and it made her smile before she could stop herself.

It was enough for Brianne to come closer and whisper something to her she wanted to believe and knew she had every reason to, even if it seemed unbelievable.

"Someone likes you."

She recalled something Brianne had said last spring after she told her about having to go to public school this year. Brianne had been looking on the bright side as usual, and Emily hadn't wanted to listen because she didn't think anyone could understand what she was going through, or that anything good could ever come out of it.

But maybe Brianne was right about God having a "surprise" waiting for her, and at the moment she felt elated at the prospect. Tyler had come to church today because of her? He couldn't wait until tomorrow to see her again? He had shouted out her name in the middle of a packed football stadium for all to hear? Why? What was going on? Who was she to attract his attention?

Brianne didn't linger and wait for her to respond to her words. But Emily found herself wishing she would have. Brianne had been a good friend at one time, but she had grown jealous of her over the last couple of years. Everyone liked Brianne. Girls, guys, the popular and unpopular. The girl with Cerebral Palsy who came in a wheelchair. The high school boy with Autism. Even Ashlee when she wasn't in one of her 'mad at the world' moods.

And Brianne loved them all right back. Love and caring and compassion and joy oozed out of her like the sweetest dessert she had ever tasted. Emily felt like a dried-up grape in comparison. And the worst part was Brianne had gone right on loving her as if they were best friends, even though they weren't.

She saw Brooke had arrived and went to say 'hi' to her. Brooke had noticed Tyler, and the first thing out of her mouth was, "What's Tyler doing here?"

"He came with Austin," she said.

"Did you talk to him yet?" Brooke asked.

"Yes."

Brooke's face lit up. "What did he say?"

Emily saw him coming their way. He was with Austin, and she nudged Brooke rather than answering. Brooke turned to look and quickly turned back, smiling at her.

He walked all the way to where they were standing and spoke to Brooke. "You go here too?"

"I do," she replied.

"I see you play piano," he said, turning his attention back to her.

"Yes," she replied.

"Me too."

"Oh? For how long?"

"About five years."

"Seven for me," she replied, but then felt dumb in saying that. "But who's counting, right?"

"You, obviously," he laughed, but it was a gracious laugh.

"Come on, Em. Time to get up there," Austin said.

She stepped away with Austin without saying anything else to Tyler. Once they started playing the first song, she mostly focused on the music, but she kept imagining Tyler watching her, and that was a strange feeling. On stage or not, she usually felt invisible.

~ CHAPTER ELEVEN ~

During the final song of the worship set, Emily debated about where to sit when she left the stage. Tyler was sitting next to Tim and Jason, but the seats on his other side were empty. She knew Austin would probably sit there, and Brianne beside him, so she didn't count on being able to sit with Tyler, and she wasn't certain she wanted to. Brooke was in the row in front of Tyler, and she often sat with Brooke on Sunday mornings, but Allie was sitting beside her, and Allie had brought a friend with her today, so there wasn't an empty seat. She wished she would have thought to put her book bag beside Brooke, like she often did, but she had forgotten because of Tyler coming to talk to them until she needed to be on stage.

The only option she had besides sitting with Brianne and Austin was to sit by herself, which she did sometimes, but to do that today would probably give Tyler the impression she was trying to avoid him, and she didn't want him to think that. Feeling indecisive when she descended the front steps and picked up her bag from where she had leaned it against the stage, she decided to go use the bathroom.

When she returned to the main room, as Pastor Nathan was finishing up with the announcements for the week, she scoped out the situation from behind the rows of chairs, but an option she hadn't expected awaited her. Austin and Brianne were sitting next to Tyler, and the seat beside Brianne was empty, but so was the one between Tyler and Austin, and she had no doubt they had left it open for her. She wanted to take one of the empty chairs near the back, but she couldn't bring herself to be antisocial today.

For all the times she had envied other girls for having boyfriends, or Brianne for having guys who liked her even if she wasn't choosing to date them yet, she knew she couldn't blow this off as no big deal. Tyler was here to see her, and rejecting that would be rude, not to mention stupid. If she didn't like him, that would be different, but she knew she did.

Feeling special to have a seat reserved for her, she stepped into the row and didn't hesitate to walk in front of Brianne and Austin to take the seat beside Tyler. He smiled at her easily, and she returned the silent greeting, trying to act natural, like this was a typical Sunday.

"I was afraid you left," Tyler whispered, leaning close to speak the words.

She didn't respond with anything besides a smile. And while she found it easy to look at Tyler and take this surprise in stride, she didn't dare look at Austin, or Brooke when she glanced back. The only person she saw was Tyler.

She listened attentively as Pastor Nathan began teaching the lesson for the morning but kept one eye on Tyler at the same time. She noticed he didn't have a

Bible with him, but she didn't try to share hers when Pastor Nathan had them turn to a place in Matthew and he read the verses out loud for them. Pastor Nathan had been their youth pastor since July, and so far she liked the way he taught. He talked about Jesus a lot, and they had been reading their way through Matthew so far. Most of the stories and series of events were familiar, but Pastor Nathan's take on them was mostly new to her. He made them more real somehow, and even with sitting beside a boy who liked her, she was still drawn to her youth pastor's words.

"Blessed are the pure in heart, for they will see God," Pastor Nathan restated from the words in chapter five. They had read several verses, but he spoke the words this time with a poetic canter. Emily had no idea what they meant, but she was intrigued.

"Let's start at the end of this phrase," he went on. *"'...for they will see God.'* Doesn't that sound cool? So far we've heard about the kingdom of heaven, being comforted, inheriting the earth, being filled, being shown mercy...and those are all well and good. But to see God? Isn't that what we long for more than anything? To see Him. To know He's real. To see this glorious Being we know He has to be? Like that song, *I Can Only Imagine.* I don't know about you, but when sing that, all kinds of images go through my mind about what I'm going to see and feel and do when I see Him for the first time; and it's never the same twice."

Emily did the same. That was one of her favorite songs.

"But wait a minute. This doesn't say, blessed are those who step through the Pearly Gates, or those who die, or those who make it to Heaven; It says 'the pure in heart.' What does that mean?"

Emily had no idea. She had been attending church her whole life, and she'd heard the words, memorized them, thought she got them, but in that moment she knew she was clueless. Pastor Nathan asked for input, and some of her peers shouted out possibilities. They all sounded plausible, and Pastor Nathan listened, nodded, and seemed to accept each answer as valid. He had his laptop hooked up to the video screen, and he typed out the answers students gave:

Righteous
Forgiven
Good
Loving
Pure Motives
Honest

"These are all good answers," he said. "And I agree. But what do they have to do with seeing God? What's the connection?"

Silence.

"Given what we know about our faith as Christians, don't you think it should say, 'Blessed are those who believe in Me (Jesus), for they will see God.'?"

Pastor Nathan left time for someone to respond, but no one did until Austin spoke out.

"To be pure in heart is to see God for who He really is, not a condition of seeing Him."

Pastor Nathan smiled. "I think someone looked at my notes before class. Were you really looking for a guitar pick in my office, Austin?"

Everyone laughed, and Austin held up his hands like he was innocent. Emily had been watchful of Austin over the past year or so. Partly because she'd had a crush on him for as long as she had been noticing boys in that way, but also because he was maturing a lot, and she was trying to figure out why. He wasn't arrogant, like he was trying to put on a show. He was quiet about it most of the time, letting his transformation be seen, more so than talking about it. And his friendship with Brianne both angered her and impressed her. His motive for hanging out with her seemed to be about truly needing her friendship, more than because he liked her.

She honestly didn't believe he had been snooping around Pastor Nathan's office. That wasn't who he was, and he wasn't trying to impress anyone with his Bible insights. He could impress everyone here with his music talent alone, and he wasn't even trying to do that.

"Where did that come from?" she heard Brianne whisper to him, and Emily wondered the same.

He shrugged. "Jesus, I guess."

Pastor Nathan went on to talk about seeing God for all He truly is, and Emily knew she needed that—a lot. She knew everything in an intellectual sense. She knew the verses and the stories and the theology, but God Himself was a mystery to her. She didn't understand Him. She wanted to love Him but didn't know how. She wanted *her* righteousness, talents, and good deeds to be noticed, more than doing anything to glorify Him.

But Austin's words and Pastor Nathan explaining them changed her thinking. She could never have a pure heart on her own, like she had been trying to do for a long time. She could only seek to know God better. And she knew the time had come to do that, but she wasn't sure how to go about it.

Pastor Nathan kept his message short and to the point, and at the end he prayed a prayer she echoed in her heart as a sincere desire.

"Help me to see you, Jesus. You are more glorious and amazing than I can ever imagine, but I want to get a fresh glimpse of you. Just a taste. Just a peek. Just a ray of your glorious light. I'm sure that's all I can handle because you are too much to take in all at once. You would blow me away with your awesomeness. So just a flash; Like lightning so powerful it would strike me dead at full strength, but from a safe distance it lights up the sky and leaves me with a sense of awe and wonder. I know you are worth loving. Worth my time. Worthy of my trust. Help me to see that."

~ CHAPTER TWELVE ~

Brianne felt compelled to reach for Austin's hand during Pastor Nate's prayer, and she did. She felt clueless about why Tyler was here, what might happen between him and Emily, and if him liking her was a good thing. But she did know she had been praying for Emily for many months now, and one way or another, this was an answer to those prayers. God was up to something, she just wasn't sure what it was, and she knew she was in for an adventurous ride; but she didn't want to go alone. She wanted her best friend by her side.

She tried to let go of his hand before the prayer ended, but Austin didn't let her, holding on until the last possible moment before those with their eyes closed around them could see the gesture of friendship that might be misinterpreted. His tight hold made her realize he was feeling the movement of Jesus among them also. And he was the one who had befriended Tyler in the first place and invited him to come today because Emily would be here. He was taking a gamble Jesus' faithfulness would prevail over any error on his part to encourage Tyler in his pursuit of Emily.

Emily, a lifetime friend of his, a church girl well-versed in the Christian faith—meets Tyler, a guy they hadn't known until five days ago and was setting foot in church for the first time today. It was a risky combination, and part of her was saying, 'No! This isn't good. This isn't what we've been praying for. This can only end badly.' But another part of her was feeling a lot of peace that God was in this, and she needed to have the faith to believe it could be a good thing.

The reality was she couldn't do a lot to influence the situation one way or the other. If Sarah was facing similar circumstances, Sarah would ask for her advice, she would give it, and Sarah would take her opinion seriously. But this was Emily, and she couldn't imagine Emily asking for her input.

So that took her back to prayer, which she had been doing. And while prayer often seemed to go unanswered and made her feel powerless, she knew God was so much bigger and powerful than her tiny mind could comprehend. Life was unpredictable, but God was faithful. She had seen that, and maybe this thing with Emily and Tyler wouldn't become anything and didn't have anything to do with her, or maybe it did.

What had Austin said? Being pure in heart was to see God for who He really is? If there was anything she wanted to see and anything God wanted to show her, she knew that was it, so the only thing to do was watch and pray and hopefully be amazed by her faithful God.

***

Pastor Nathan always ended the teaching by ten-thirty, giving them plenty of time to hang out before the main church service began in the other building at eleven o'clock. Some sat around and talked. Others played basketball or air hockey or foosball. Emily didn't usually hang around for more than ten minutes. If she was working in the nursery or toddler room, she needed to be there by 10:45, and if she wasn't, she would go sit in the main sanctuary of the church and wait for her family to join her.

Today she didn't need to rush off. Remaining in her seat, she waited to see what Tyler and the others did, and within two minutes it was just her and Tyler sitting there talking, and he admitted something.

"This is the first time I've ever been to church. Do you always come here on Sundays?"

"Yes," she replied. "Every week for as long as I can remember, unless I've been sick or my family is out of town."

"Do you like that?"

"Mmmm, mostly. Sometimes I feel bored with it and would rather stay home and sleep in, but now that we have the band going, it's been okay."

"Do your parents make you come, or could you stay home if you want?"

"I don't know," she said. "I've never asked them."

He didn't respond to that, and she asked him something.

"How did you like it?"

"It was fine, I guess. Kind of like school only with singing and prayer too."

She wasn't sure how to respond to that, so she didn't. She felt uncertain about what to say next, or how to handle having a boy like her who didn't attend church. In her mind she was thinking, 'I can't do this. He likes me, but I need to discourage him in that and act uninterested.' But she didn't know how without being rude or her usual reclusive self. And something was telling her to not be that way.

"Are you glad you came?" she asked, wondering if being in an unfamiliar setting was worth it to him, or if he would rather keep their interaction limited to the school bus.

He smiled. "I really wanted to see you before tomorrow."

"Why?"

He laughed and sounded nervous. "I'm not sure. I just did."

She smiled.

"Are you glad I'm here?"

She wasn't sure how to respond. Casually like, 'Yeah, sure. Whatever.' Or more dreamy. 'I love that you're here.' Sigh. Or somewhere in the middle.

"I am," she replied. "I'm surprised, but it's a good surprise."

"Do you think we could go out sometime? Like to the movies next Friday, or this afternoon?"

She laughed. He was surprising her, but not in an uncomfortable way. He was being honest and not making her guess his intentions. But she had to be honest too.

"I think I'd like that," she replied, "but my parents won't let me date yet."

He didn't seem shocked by that. "Can I see you at all outside of school?"

"We're not in school now."

"Okay. Outside of school and here?"

"I don't know," she replied. "I'd have to ask. You could probably come over to my house as long as my parents are there."

"You do live on my street, so that would be easy."

"Just promise you'll never try to walk there."

"It's not that far," he said.

"I know, but that one corner just before your driveway—you know the one with the deep ditch on one side and the hillside on the other."

"Yeah."

"A few years ago a boy was killed there. He was walking on the shoulder, but a car came around the corner and hit him. It was so sad."

"Did you know him?"

"Sort of. We knew the family, but their kids were older. He was fourteen at the time. I was in sixth grade."

"Okay, I won't walk," he said. "I'm sure my parents can drive me."

She wasn't certain her mom and dad would want him coming to their house and them spending time together, but she would ask, and if she couldn't see him outside of school or church, that would be okay. So far she'd only spent time with him on the bus and here and felt comfortable with both. She just hoped he wouldn't lose interest or feel so limited by her parents' rules he decided she wasn't worth it.

She decided it would be a good idea for her parents to meet him today since he was here, and she knew where they both were, so she asked him if he wanted to meet them now.

"Sure," he said.

"Were you planning to stay for the church service?"

"There's another one?"

She smiled. "In the other building. Austin's family usually stays."

"I guess I am then," he replied.

She put her Bible into her bag, stood up, and slung it over her shoulder. He got up also, and she led the way to the doors in the back. Along the way they passed Austin, and Tyler said he would be with her, which Austin didn't question or ask for more details on. Going outside and crossing the open pathway between the two buildings, they walked side-by-side and stepped into the side door of the main church at the base of the stairs that went to the upper floor.

Both of her parents taught classes upstairs, but her dad was more likely to be finished. Her mom had to wait for parents to pick up their kids, and it would be noisy and chaotic. Emily saw the adults in her dad's class coming out of the room as they approached the end of the hall, and several of them said hello to her, including one couple she babysat for regularly, and they asked if she could still come on Tuesday evening.

"Yes, I'll be there," she replied.

She saw several of the adults glance at Tyler as she spoke to them, and they all knew it was unusual to see her with a boy unless it was a whole group of them. But no one said anything, and they eventually made it into the classroom. Her dad was talking to one of the older couples who attended his class and Emily knew well. Mr. and Mrs. Kerns were a sweet couple that had their family over for dinner several times a year, and she decided to hang back until they stepped away, or she would end up introducing Tyler to them also, and that would be awkward. Even introducing him to her dad was going to be interesting, and she suddenly wasn't sure why she had decided to do this.

She glanced at Tyler, wondering if he would rather do this some other time, but he didn't seem to care about anything except being with her. He smiled at her, and she smiled back.

"Are you sure this is okay?" she said quietly, feeling certain her dad hadn't spotted them yet.

"Sure," he shrugged, reaching for her fingers and brushing them gently. He didn't hold her hand, but it was a deliberate display of affection, and she felt something unique at his touch.

Turning back to look at her dad, she saw Mr. and Mrs. Kerns were stepping away. The older couple spotted her as they came toward the door, and she smiled and said 'hello'. They returned the greeting, and she stepped forward to give Mrs. Kerns a hug.

"How are you, dear?"

"I'm fine," she replied. "How are you?"

"Good, good. We were just telling your dad we won't be here for a few weeks because we're leaving on our trip tomorrow."

"Where are you going?"

"To see our kids. Janice in Spokane first and then Gary in Boise."

"I hope you have a nice time."

"Thank you, dear. I'm sure we will."

They stepped past her, and she saw them glance at Tyler on their way out, but they didn't say anything to him, and when she looked toward her dad, she saw he had noticed her, and his attention remained on her as she stepped toward him with Tyler at her side.

Her heart started pounding really hard, but she went through with her plans, introducing Tyler to her dad first and then her dad to Tyler, feeling sort of robotic about it, but it got the job done.

"Good to meet you, Tyler," her dad said, reaching out to shake his hand.

"Good to meet you, sir," Tyler replied, and Emily wondered how many times he had done this—meeting a girl's parents he was interested in. He didn't seem nervous enough for it to be his first time, and Emily wondered if she was being stupid, thinking Tyler saw her as something special but actually did this all the time, meeting the parents of whatever girl he was dating that week.

In reality she knew very little about Tyler, but she hadn't thought about that until now, and it was too late to backtrack, so she waited to see how her dad handled this from here.

"Have you been attending youth group here for awhile?"

"No," Tyler replied. "My family and I moved here last month, and this is my first time."

Her dad appeared puzzled by that, and Emily felt the need to explain, saying Tyler was a friend of Austin's and he lived a half-mile from them on Hazel Grove Road.

"Oh, I see," her dad replied. "Welcome to Clatskanie, Tyler. Is your whole family here?"

"No. Just me."

"We've got a good thing going here with the new building and hiring a full time youth pastor. We could give you a ride whenever you need that. Hazel Grove is a bit out of the Lockhart's way."

Emily hadn't thought of that, and she didn't have a problem with giving Tyler a ride to church, but all of this seemed unreal to her at the moment, like it was happening to someone else, especially when Tyler spoke again and left her dad momentarily speechless.

"I was talking to Emily about coming over to the house sometimes too. Would that be all right?"

"After church, you mean?"

"Yes, and other times if Emily doesn't get tired of me—we can study together, or whatever."

Tyler looked at her and smiled when he said the last part, and Emily felt shocked he would be so bold. If Tyler had any reservations about how much he liked her at this point, he wasn't showing it.

Her dad responded diplomatically, but he wasn't clueless about what was going on, and Emily saw a side of him she hadn't before.

"We can talk about that," he said. "How about if we start with lunch after church today and go from there?"

Tyler glanced at her again. "Is that all right with you, Emily?"

"Sure," she replied, looking into those captivating green eyes and feeling really special. She had no idea why this was happening, but it was definitely happening.

~ CHAPTER THIRTEEN ~

Brooke stepped into the main church sanctuary and scanned the large room. She was looking for Emily, and she spotted her in the usual place. Emily's mom and dad always wanted Emily and her sisters to sit with them as a family, but sometimes Brooke sat with them. Seeing Tyler was occupying the space beside Emily this morning, she smiled and decided to leave them be. She wasn't surprised a guy was finally taking notice of Emily, and she suspected Tyler wasn't the first, just one bold enough to do something about it. But she was surprised how easily Emily was handling Tyler's interest.

Going to sit with Brianne instead, she resisted the urge to talk about the big news of the morning and asked Brianne how she was doing. They talked for at least a minute before one of them finally mentioned Emily, and it was Brianne who said something.

"Has Emily said anything to you about Tyler?"

Brooke explained about being at the football game and Tyler giving Emily the note. Brianne knew about Emily being at the football game, but she didn't know she had gone with Brooke.

"That's why she was there!" Brianne said. "I couldn't figure out why she would have gone to the game if she hates going to public school so much."

"I invited her, and I was surprised when she said yes. I think she was bored until she got the note, but you should have seen the look on her face!"

They both laughed. Brooke didn't turn to look at Emily because she didn't want her to know they were talking about her. Emily could get embarrassed easily, but when Brooke glanced her direction a few times during worship, Emily seemed to be focused on what was going on up front, and Tyler was too. Brooke didn't know if Tyler usually attended church, but he looked comfortable enough. All week at school he'd been quiet, but at the football game and here this morning with Emily he had been completely different.

She only had a brief chance to talk to Emily afterwards and learned Tyler was going home with them, having lunch with her family, and then who knew? Emily whispered the information while Tyler was talking to Austin about leaving with Emily instead of going to his house for the afternoon like they planned.

"Have fun!" she whispered back. "Call me later."

Emily smiled and seemed nervous about what the rest of the day might hold, but she didn't admit it verbally. Brooke's family didn't hang around too long after church, so she went to find her parents and was looking forward to going out for lunch like they usually did. On the drive there, Brooke wondered what it would be like to have a boy showing that kind of interest in her, but she couldn't imagine it. She liked Jason and always got a flutter in her stomach when she was around him, but to actually have him riding along in the car to have Sunday lunch with her family—she didn't expect that to happen anytime soon, and in reality she wasn't sure she wanted it to. Maybe when they were older, but for today it was nothing more than wishful thinking.

She heard from Emily sooner than she was expecting. Emily called at two-thirty, and Tyler had been there for lunch, but her dad took him home afterwards. Her mom and dad wanted to discuss the issue of them spending time together before they made a decision on the matter, which really didn't surprise Emily, but she was upset by it. She felt like her parents had been rude to Tyler when they told him matter-of-factly he needed to go home.

Brooke understood her feelings but saw her parents' point of view too. They had just met the guy today, and they were protective of their daughters. "Don't worry about it, Em. If Tyler likes you and he's a guy worth getting to know, he'll understand and respect their wishes."

"But what if they don't want me to spend any time with him outside of school and church?"

"Respect their decision and it will work out. Sometimes my parents say things I don't like, but then later I see they were right. They want the best for you. There are worse things in life than having a mom and dad who care about you. Just ask Allie about that."

"I know," she sighed.

"It was cool how he came to church to see you! What kind of guy does that?"

Emily laughed. "I don't know. I can't believe he was there."

"After talking to him on Friday night, I wasn't surprised."

***

Emily tried to remain optimistic after talking to Brooke, but she had no idea how her parents were going to handle this. She'd been hopeful at church when her dad met Tyler and invited him to have lunch here, but after they got home his mood seemed more cautious, lunch had been awkward, and then suddenly it was, 'Okay, I'm taking you home now, Tyler,' and it wasn't up for discussion. She'd barely had a chance to say good-bye to him before he was out the door.

She came up to her room to call Brooke on her cell phone, which she wasn't supposed to be doing. They had gotten her a prepaid phone for emergencies only, and it didn't work downstairs because of the location of their house and surrounding tall trees. But she could get a signal here in her room she had discovered one day when she checked it after school to see if it needed to be charged.

Her mom was downstairs, and she expected her mom and dad to have a discussion when her dad returned, so she laid on her bed with her vampire book to keep reading. She had spent most of her spare time yesterday finishing up *20,000 Leagues Under The Sea* after getting started on Friday afternoon.

While she waited for her parents to come up and talk to her at some point, she resisted the urge to call Tyler. He had given her his phone number on the drive here, and she had given him hers—the one for the house, not her cell phone. She hadn't given that number to anyone because her friends weren't supposed to call or text her on it anyway, and she hadn't seen any reason to give it to Tyler until after lunch when she suddenly got the impression her mom and dad might not be keen on her spending time with him.

Last weekend when her parents had given her the phone and explained what it was for, she hadn't had any desire to use it for anything besides emergencies. But now a week later, things had changed, and she felt like it was her one connection to the outside world from the prison of her room her parents had confined her to.

Actually, she had confined herself because she didn't want to be downstairs right now, and in reality if she wanted to go downstairs and use the landline to call any of her friends, even Tyler, they weren't going to stop her.

Feeling mixed-up, confused, and out of control of her negative emotions, she closed her book she couldn't concentrate on anyway and opened her weary heart to God. This morning she had asked Him to reveal Himself to her, and she wanted that, but since leaving church she had shut out any thought of Him.

"I don't know what to do, Jesus," she whispered, letting the tears come. "What am I supposed to do? What if Mom and Dad say I can't see Tyler except at school and church? What if he doesn't like that and decides it's not worth it? What if I can see him, but in a few weeks he stops wanting to? Does he do this often? Am I just another girl to him, or does he see me as being as special as he makes me feel when he looks at me? Should I be doing this now? I'm fourteen. Should I ignore boys until I'm done with high school? Just be friends with them? Should I even be considering spending time with Tyler if he's not a Christian? What if we get along well and I really like him and we have fun together but he doesn't have any interest in You?"

She felt better getting all those questions out in the open, but she didn't hear God answer any of them yet. Going back to her reading, she had read about half a page when someone knocked on her door.

"Come in," she called out, laying her book aside with the cover face down. Her mom and dad didn't monitor her reading material that carefully, but she didn't imagine they would look too fondly on her current choice.

It was her mom, which didn't surprise her too much. Her mom was usually the spokesperson for her parents' decisions, and she didn't consider her solitary presence to be a good or bad sign, just the way it was. Her mom sat down on the edge of her bed and patted her leg like she was eight. Her expression didn't give anything away, and Emily waited for her to speak, feeling prepared for the worst but hoping for something else.

"Your dad and I talked it over, and we decided it would be fine for Tyler to come here for lunch on Sundays, and also for him to come on Saturdays or in the evenings sometimes as long as we're here and you don't have a lot of homework."

She was surprised. "Really?"

"If that's what you want," her mom said, sort of like when she had given her choices regarding her homeschooling, only this was about a social issue instead of an educational one.

She thought seriously for a moment. Tyler had been the one to ask if he could see her outside of school and church, and she hadn't been opposed to it, but she realized she hadn't thought seriously about what she wanted. And she supposed she couldn't know fully unless he was here a few times and she saw what their time together was like. But if their times together so far were an accurate indication, she thought it would be nice.

"Yeah, I think I'd like that," she replied.

Her mom smiled, but it was a cautious smile, and Emily made her a promise she felt she could keep.

"If I don't like spending time with him, I'll let Daddy run him off and tell him to never come back."

Her mom laughed, but she warned her of something also. "Sometimes it can be hard to stop seeing someone once you start, even if it's not going well."

She knew her mom was speaking from experience on that. Before she married her dad, her mom had an unhealthy relationship with someone. Remembering Brooke's words about her mom and dad wanting to protect her, she knew that was a blessing, and she also knew having to stop homeschooling had been as hard for her mom as it was for her. She gave her mom a hug.

"Thanks for saying it's okay," she said. "I'll try to be honest with myself about it, and you and dad."

"I don't know if I'm ready for you to be fourteen yet."

"I'll try to remember I'm only fourteen. I think I'm going to come up with my own list of conditions by the time Tyler comes again," she said, suddenly feeling grateful he wasn't here right now. All of this was happening really fast, and she needed time to think about what she wanted.

After her mom left, she took some paper from her desk and made a list of things she wanted to discuss with Tyler, or at least think about seriously. She wasn't certain what she wanted concerning some of it, but she left everything open before God and asked Him to give her direction.

She didn't expect Him to speak so quickly, but His voice was unmistakable, and she knew if she was going to take the right steps on this uncertain path, she needed to start with what He was telling her to do today.

~ CHAPTER FOURTEEN ~

Brianne was working on her scrapbook in her bedroom when her mom poked her head in the open doorway to tell her she had a phone call. Getting up from her workspace, she went to the kitchen to take the call, not expecting it to be any particular person, but feeling surprised it was Emily. Emily used to call her once in awhile, but Brianne couldn't remember the last time.

"Hey, Em. What's up?"

"I need to talk to you," she said hesitantly. "Is this a good time?"

"Sure."

Feeling this might be a private conversation, she wandered out of the kitchen toward the front porch where she could speak more freely. She almost asked if this was about Tyler, but she didn't want to speculate anything at this point.

"I need your advice," Emily said before she got out of the house.

Brianne was shocked, but she tried not to show it. "About what?"

"Tyler. How do you do it—be Austin's girlfriend but not really?"

Brianne liked that description of their relationship, but she was surprised Emily saw it that way. Emily generally gave her the impression she didn't believe they were "just friends".

"Is that what you want? To be Tyler's girlfriend, but not really?"

"I'm not sure yet," Emily replied. "I'm just wondering how you do it."

Brianne took her request seriously, and she thought about what made her friendship with Austin work, and she knew it was a few key things.

"First we're friends before anything else. We talk. We have fun together. We help each other through stuff. We talk about our relationships with family members, and other friends, and God. And we enjoy all of that for what it is."

She paused and asked Emily something. "Do you feel you can talk to Tyler easily, or are you tongue-tied around him?"

"I can talk to him. Which surprises me, but whenever he's around, it just happens."

"That's the way it is with me and Austin too. He's not a girl, but I talk with him as easily as I do with you or Brooke or Sarah. That's pretty much how we became close friends in the first place, and that's never changed."

"I can't usually talk to guys," Emily admitted. "Even guys like Austin I've known for a long time."

"I'm still that way with some, but not Austin or Joel. Don't ask me why, I'm just not."

"I think I know the answer to this, and you don't have to answer if you don't want to, but have you ever kissed Austin?"

Brianne smiled. "What do you think?"

"No."

"You're right. I've never kissed anyone."

"Do you think I can do this with Tyler and not have us kiss and stuff?"

"Is that what you want?"

"I don't think I'm ready, and if he's used to kissing girls he's spending that kind of time with, I don't want to be another one, you know?"

"It's fine for you to tell him what you want your relationship to be about. All you can do is be honest and see what happens. How he responds is a big clue of what he's really like and if he's someone you want as a friend."

"Assuming he's nice, why does he like me, Brianne? I don't get it."

"I can think of a lot of reasons why he would like you, but the only way to know what he's thinking is to ask him."

"Do you think I should do that?"

"Yes, I do."

Emily sighed.

"I know this is what everyone always says, but it's true: Just be yourself, Emily. Isn't that what you've been doing so far?"

"Yes."

"It's working. He came to church to see you. He asked you out. He was willing to go home with you when that's all you could offer him. He likes you, Emily."

"I like him too," she admitted.

Brianne didn't think she could give her any further advice for the moment. Maybe things would continue to progress, or maybe by next weekend Emily would be saying he was a jerk, but Brianne knew of one thing she could say, and she said it.

"I'm here for you, Em. Whenever you need to talk, okay? I've depended on my friends when I've been unsure or confused or needed to talk something out, and I'm here if you need that from me."

"I know you are," she said softly. "I'm sorry I've been a brat sometimes. It's not you. I've been feeling—I don't know. Like growing up is harder than I thought it would be."

"I know the feeling," she replied. "And it is hard, so we can't shut out our friends. Our real friends."

"Are you going to try out for the play at school?"

"I was thinking I might, but I don't know if I'm good enough."

"You are, Brianne. You're a really good actress, and you sing well. You should try out. I will too, and maybe we'll both get a part and can practice together."

"Okay," she said, not feeling entirely certain she wanted to try out for the play, but not wanting to tell her no either. It had been too long since Emily had responded to any of her attempts at friendship to brush this off and wait for the next time. "And if I don't get a part, but you do, I'll still help you with your lines if you want me to—unless of course you can get Tyler to do that."

They both laughed.

They talked for a long time, about school and youth group and their families and the possibility of moving into a larger house. She hadn't had a chance to tell Emily, and Emily agreed they needed more space.

"I'd like to have a group of friends over more often, but it's hard to do that here. I'm hoping for something with a cool basement, or a large bonus room like Brooke's house has."

"It's weird for me to think about living anywhere besides here," Emily said. "I was too young when we moved to remember."

Emily couldn't talk much longer after that. Her parents had rules about how long she and her sisters could be on the phone, but Brianne felt elated Emily had called her, and she almost called Austin to share the promising news with him. But sitting there on the porch in the afternoon sun with a mild fall breeze tossing the ends of her hair, and the beauty surrounding her she had rediscovered yesterday, she shared her thoughts with God instead.

That was cool, Jesus. You always surprise me when I least expect it. I hope getting to know Tyler and spending time with him can be a good thing for Emily, and for Tyler too. I hope he can come to know you in a real way. A way that changes his present and his future. A way you've had planned for him all along.

~ CHAPTER FIFTEEN ~

Emily felt nervous about seeing Tyler on Monday morning. She had thought he might call her yesterday, but he never did. She was worried after meeting her parents and realizing this might be more complicated than he had imagined, Tyler had decided she wasn't worth it. But when he wasn't at his stop, she wondered if he was sick today, and that seemed to be the case when she didn't see him in P.E. first period, nor in science two hours later. After she got home from school, she called him, and he answered, but he sounded awful.

"Are you sick?"

"Yes," he coughed. "I've been sleeping all day."

"You were fine yesterday."

"I know. It came on really fast."

"Is it the flu?" she cringed. She really didn't want to get sick.

"I think it might be," he said. "Sorry. I hope you don't get it."

"I hope you feel better soon," she replied. "I have some good news. Would you like to hear it?"

"Sure," he said.

"My mom and dad said it's okay for you to come over sometimes. As long as they're here and I don't have too much homework."

"That's good news," he said. "Really, Emily."

He coughed more and made a sound like he was shivering.

"Do you have a fever?"

"Yes, but I feel cold."

"Is your mom or dad there?"

"They both had to work today. But my mom is coming home soon."

"I'd come take care of you, but I have to stay here with my sisters."

"I wouldn't let you anyway," he said.

"Because you don't want me to get sick?"

"That and I don't want you walking here either."

She smiled. She had forgotten about telling him that yesterday.

He coughed again, and she said she would let him go, but he didn't want her to.

"Just talk to me. I'll listen."

"About what?"

"Your day."

"It wasn't very exciting."

"It had to be better than mine."

She supposed that was true, so she went ahead and began with P.E. and gave him a run-down of her day. She told him what they had done in science and math, but she didn't bother giving him the homework information. He wouldn't be up for doing any of it yet.

"Is someone there with you now?" she asked when she heard talking in the background.

"My mom just got home."

"Okay. I'm glad you're not alone anymore."

"I haven't been alone since you called me."

She smiled. He was so sweet. And she didn't think he could fake that, especially when he was sick.

"I'm going to let you go now," she said. "But I'll call you later, okay?"

"Okay. I doubt I'll be at school tomorrow."

"Get some rest. I hope you feel better."

"Thanks. Me too."

She almost said she would pray for him, but she decided not to and just prayed for him after she hung up the phone. She found it surprising she cared about him so much already. It was a strange feeling, considering the little amount of time she had known him.

***

When Sarah received Brianne's letter on Wednesday, she was happy to get a real letter from her again, especially after she read it and remembered how Brianne wrote when she had things on her heart she wanted to share. Receiving her emails every day had been great and made her feel more connected to her on a daily basis, but Brianne put her heart into handwritten letters more, and Sarah had missed that. She knew she was the same way and Brianne might need a longer letter from her as well, so she wrote her one after dinner.

Dear Brianne,

Thanks for your letter. I loved it! I've missed hearing from you in that way, and I wanted to write you back and share more from my heart also. Let's see, where should I begin?

First I think it's cool Emily is getting to know a new guy at your school and you and Austin are praying he comes to know Jesus. As I said in the email I wrote you yesterday, I will be praying for that too, and for Emily. I feel like I know what to pray for after being in a relationship with Ryan that became more exclusive than I was ready for. And speaking of Ryan, I want to ask for your prayers because he's been emailing me regularly since we moved, and I'm starting to consider the possibility God might be keeping him in my life for a significant purpose. Yesterday he said something in his email about how much he misses me, and I wasn't opposed to him feeling that way. I'm not sure what that means, just pray for us.

We have our first league volleyball match tomorrow, and I'm excited. We have a really good team. Our coach has been helping me with my serve, and I've gotten a lot better since last week. She wants to see us improve and learn how to play better, not just expect us to work harder and fight for a spot on the starting lineup. It seems more fun this year, even though Annalise had to quit the team and she's my best friend here so far. I still see her a lot though. She's coming to youth group with me again tonight, so that should be fun.

I didn't want to ask you this right away, and I didn't want to email you about it because I don't want you giving me a quick response back, but on Sunday I found out our youth group is going on a retreat next month. We're going to a place near Vernonia, so I know it would be easy for you to meet us there, but I only want you to come if you feel like God wants you to, not just me. (But I really hope you can!)

I still miss you, Brianne, and I hope the day will come when we can see each other more often than a few times a year. I don't know why God has me here, but I'm trusting He has His reasons. I do think you should try out for the school play, and I'll come see it if you have a part.

Miss you,
Sarah

After putting the letter into an envelope and writing Brianne's address on the front, she checked her email and had a message from Brianne about her day, and she also had another message from Ryan.

Hi, Sarah. How was your day? Mine was okay. I had to go to the library during my study period to do some research online, and it reminded me of when we first met. That seems like a long time ago.

I hope I didn't upset you by what I said yesterday. I know you don't want a boyfriend right now, or for anything to happen between us with you living in another city, but I hope we can still be close friends by writing back and forth several times a week. Girls like you are hard to find, Sarah, and even the guy-friends I have aren't exactly deep-thinkers. I try to be a normal teen guy who plays sports and video games and asks one girl to the dance this week and another the next, but I can't do it. I go crazy without some kind of deep connection with at least one other person, and you've always been that person for me. I talk to you like I can't talk to my other friends.

Well, there I went again, giving you my sorry story and begging for your friendship. If you don't write me back, I'll take the hint, and it's okay, Sarah. Really. I'm just letting you know what you mean to me and how much I miss you, but if you don't feel the same way, it's okay. I'll live, and I know Jesus will carry me and bring some other beautiful girl my way one of these days :)

Sarah smiled. She couldn't help it. Ryan was a sweetheart. He had been nothing but good to her. A good boyfriend during the few months she had defined him that way. And a good friend since then, even though he had been hurt by her decision to end things between them in a romantic way.

Ever since leaving Clatskanie before her seventh-grade year, she had been asking God for a best friend like Brianne, and Ryan had come closer to that than anyone else. She wished now she had just been friends with him like Brianne was with Austin so they wouldn't have gone through the drama of "breaking-up", which wasn't how she would define it, but that's what it felt like and the way Ryan had taken it.

But she also knew she had allowed their relationship to develop into something beyond friendship because he was special and she needed it at the time. One of the reasons she had ended things between them in that way was because she felt like she was spending too much time with him and closing herself off from developing other friendships, but after they stopped being boyfriend and girlfriend, she hadn't spent a significant amount of time with any particular friends, and then she had moved away from the few she had anyway.

She'd been hopeful of making good friends here, and she had, but she still didn't have that one special friend like Brianne had always been. And she knew the same was true about Ryan. The only benefit she could see as a result of breaking up with him was looking back on it all now and realizing what they'd had didn't come along every day, and she knew she missed it. She missed him. She needed exactly what he was describing as needing for himself, and she was tired of trying to be strong about something she didn't need to be strong about.

She didn't have time to write him back at the moment because she needed to get her homework done before youth group, but he was on her mind for the rest of the evening, and before she went to bed she decided to write out her thoughts to him in a longhand letter.

Dear Ryan,

I'm sorry I haven't responded to your emails this week, but I've been thinking a lot about what you said, and I've come to the conclusion I feel the same way. I miss you. I miss our talks. I miss seeing you at school and church. I've tried to replace your friendship and brush it off as something I needed for a time and that time has ended, but it hasn't. Other than Brianne, you're the best friend I've ever had, and if Brianne and I can still be close, I know we can be too. If you're willing to put the effort into us again, so am I.

It's funny how we get ideals into our head about how life is supposed to work and then see God doing things that don't fit into those plans. But I think sometimes we have to live that way to see our plans are just that: our own. This growing-up stuff is so complicated! But you and I have only been complicated when I've made it complicated. I'm sorry, Ryan. Why are you even thinking about me after all this time?

I'm happy to have you as a close friend from a distance, and I know that's all it can be right now, but I would like to see you sometime soon if possible.

If you want to call me when you get this, you can. But if you landed another girlfriend this week while you thought I stopped speaking to you, it's my loss, Ryan.

I wanted to say this in an old-fashioned letter instead of clicking on the send button in an email, because I know if I see it all the way through to writing your address on the envelope, putting a stamp on it, and walking it to the neighborhood mailbox, then this is what I really want. So if you're holding this, it is.

Love,
Sarah

~ CHAPTER SIXTEEN ~

Brianne was in a good mood when she arrived for youth group on Thursday evening. Sarah had sent her an email from school during lunch, saying she was bursting at the seams to tell her about the letter she had mailed to Ryan. Brianne wasn't opposed to Sarah "getting back to the core of their friendship", as she put it. And she could see a long-distance thing working for them.

Her joy only increased when she saw Emily and Tyler come in together a few minutes after she arrived. She knew Tyler had been sick all week, but she hadn't heard how he was doing since talking to Emily last night during the children's midweek program they both helped with. Emily had talked to him after school, and he sounded better but didn't think he would be at school today, and he hadn't been. Stepping over to say 'hi', she gave Emily a hug and told Tyler it was good to see him and asked how he was feeling.

"Better," he said. "Not quite up for marching band practice, but it's good to be out of the house."

She almost said, 'And to see Emily?' But he beat her to it. Emily smiled at him, and Brianne saw a definite difference in Emily when she was around Tyler. On

Sunday it had been, 'Is he really looking at me like that?' Today it was an acceptance of the fact, and she seemed less self-conscious than usual. More at peace. More herself.

Emily warmed up with the rest of the band on stage, and during the ten minutes when everyone else was arriving, Emily went to sit with Tyler and they talked quietly with one another until it was time for her to leave his side. Brianne was trying not to stare, but she kept glancing their way because they were so watchable, and they were in their own little world, so neither of them noticed her spying.

She was on stage, waiting for the others to join her, when Emily got up from her seat, but Tyler didn't let her go without grasping her hand and holding it gently until the last possible moment. As Emily walked toward her, Brianne waited for her to make eye-contact, and when she did, Emily smiled as she suddenly connected with another human being besides the one who had been occupying her thoughts for the past ten minutes.

Emily walked past her at first, giving her a smile but not saying anything, but while they were waiting for Austin and Pastor Nate to get up there, Emily stepped over from the keyboard and whispered something in her ear.

"What is he doing here?"

Brianne smiled at her. "He's here to be with you, Em."

"No," she replied. "That's not possible!"

Brianne found herself praying for Tyler all through worship. She knew him being here tonight wasn't an accident. Whether Tyler knew it or not, Jesus was making Himself known, and she prayed Tyler would see it. He should be at marching band practice tonight, but he wasn't because he'd been sick this week. And he hadn't wanted to move here, but he'd found a reason to like it. She didn't know exactly how some people saw God reaching into their world and others totally missed it, but she prayed with all of her heart Tyler's eyes would be wide open to the obvious.

By eight o'clock he looked ready to go home, as she would expect after him being sick all week, but he didn't seem in a hurry to get out of here. Emily's dad had a meeting tonight that was supposed to be over by eight, but he didn't come in to let Emily know he was ready until eight-fifteen, giving Brianne and Austin extra time to chat with them. Austin and Tyler had become friends in a short amount of time last week, and Tyler's interest in Emily didn't seem to be taking away from that at all.

"How long have you been playing guitar, Austin?" Tyler asked.

"Three years."

"Do you have any interest in starting a band?"

"I've thought about it," Austin said. "But this keeps me pretty busy."

"You'd make a good lead singer," Tyler said. "Do you write songs?"

Brianne smiled and met Austin's amused expression. "A bit," he replied.

"He's being modest," Emily said. "He writes really good songs."

"You've got a good bass player and Mike can shred on the electric. Who's the kid drumming?"

"That's J.T.," Austin replied. "Brianne's little brother. He's doing all right, but he hasn't been playing long."

"I could drum for you, if you want to go for it sometime."

Brianne didn't know Tyler played the drums, and apparently Austin didn't either.

"Dude! Seriously?"

"I took lessons for two years, and I play around with it on my own. I hear the band playing in my head, but—"

"We should get together and jam," Austin said. "See what we can do."

"I'm cool with that," Tyler replied. "Can we practice here?"

"My dad has a key. If we can find a time we're all free, I'd say it's worth a shot."

***

Emily thought some of the guys starting a band was a cool idea. She knew Tyler was right about Austin making a good lead singer, and he played guitar well. She hadn't known Tyler knew how to play drums either, and she knew it would be a good thing for him to have a reason to hang around with Austin and the other guys in the band. She didn't think about herself and how she might fit into it all too, until they were riding home in the back seat of her dad's car and Tyler brought it up again.

"Have you written any songs, Emily?"

She smiled. Up until a few weeks ago no one had ever asked her that, and her song notebook had been something she had never mentioned or shown to anyone, but while they were at camp, Austin asked her

142

out-of-the-blue, and she admitted her secret to him. Now Tyler was asking too? How weird was that?

"Did Austin tell you?"

"Austin? No. Why, do you?"

"Yes, but no one knows that except him—and probably Brianne too."

He reached for her hand and held it in the space between them. He'd done the same on the way to the church earlier. "Why not?" he asked.

"It's not something I share with people."

"Will you share them with me? I mean, can I hear one sometime?"

"Maybe," she replied, not wanting to commit to that. Austin knew she wrote songs, but he hadn't asked to hear them. "I'm better with the lyrics than the music. What I write sounds like other songs I've heard, just with different words."

"I'm better at the music," he said. "It's the lyrics I can't come up with. Maybe we could work on something together—something to share with the band."

She giggled. "My lyrics might be too girly for a boy band."

"A boy band? No, thank you. If we sound like a boy band, I'm quitting."

She laughed. "I just meant Austin might not want to sing the kind of words I write."

"So you sing them, and we'll back you up."

"I don't think so."

"Why not? You sing. We'll just put a microphone on you. Can you play piano and sing at the same time?"

"Yes," she replied. "But I'm not going to be—"

She stopped and looked at him.

"You didn't mean for me to be in the band."

"Of course I did. Three guitarists and a drummer isn't a band. We're going to need keyboard. And some girl vocals will be good too. Between you and Brianne, we'd be set."

"Marissa is a better singer than me," she said, not feeling opposed to playing keyboard for the band but not seeing herself as a major vocal presence. She was classically trained, not a rocker.

"Who's Marissa?"

"She leads worship sometimes. She plays guitar too."

"Do you think she'd want to be in the band?"

"Maybe."

"We'll figure it out as we go along," he said, seeming intent on making this work. "When would be a good time for you to be at practice?"

She thought about her schedule. It wasn't as busy as it used to be when she was taking three dance classes and had voice and piano lessons too. Now she had one dance class on Tuesday afternoons, and she had voice lessons on Saturday morning. They had worship band practice on Saturday afternoons, but if they were already there, they could practice afterwards, she supposed. Or sometime on Sunday would be okay too. The only weeknight that might work was Monday.

She shared the possibilities with him, and he said those times were fine for him too. She wasn't sure Austin had been thinking she would be a part of the band, but she couldn't imagine him not wanting her to if she showed up. Being the only girl, however, could be interesting, and she decided to ask Brianne on Friday if she was planning to sing with them.

"I wasn't really thinking that," Brianne said when she talked to her before their choir teacher started class. "But maybe Austin was. I'll ask him."

"Do you think it's dumb for me to be in the band?"

"Why would I think that?" Brianne laughed. "You're the most talented musician we have. It would be dumb to not have you!"

Emily wasn't sure why she didn't see herself as talented. She knew she had the skills because she practiced a lot, but she didn't see herself as being gifted.

The fall play castings were posted after school, and she got one of the roles she was hoping for, and she was shocked to see her name on there a second time as an understudy for the lead female role.

"Emily!" Brianne screamed, standing beside her and seeing it as well.

She smiled and laughed, but she felt dazed. She hadn't gotten her hopes up about getting a part at all. She was excited about being in the play, but she wouldn't have been that disappointed if she hadn't made it, especially since she was only a ninth grader.

Both Brianne and Austin had gotten small parts. Austin was listed as a "street boy", and Brianne was the "dress merchant". Emily didn't know if either of them had lines or were just random chorus members, and neither did they. But they were fine with their minor roles and excited for her.

They didn't have much time before they needed to catch the bus, so they stepped away to head out the side door close to where the busses lined up. But once they were out of the mob of others trying to see the cast listings, Brianne grabbed her and gave her a hug.

"I'm so excited for you, Emily. Congratulations!"

"Thanks," she said, not feeling surprised by Brianne's words or warm emotion because she was always encouraging and sweet.

But when Austin didn't let her get away before giving her a hug and speaking genuine words, something inside of her woke up to the reality she had accomplished something truly noteworthy. Something she was gifted to do.

"I'm not surprised, Emily," he said. "You're going to do great."

"Thank you," she whispered.

They walked out of the building side-by-side, and Austin said something else. "Tyler told me he thought you should be a part of the band, and I agree. We need you, Emily. Will you join us?"

She had one condition to saying yes. "As long as I'm not the only girl."

"I don't sing without Brianne, so you won't be."

"I think we should talk to Marissa too," Emily added. "She's got the best rocker-girl voice."

"That's true," Brianne said.

"Seven band members sounds like a good number to me," Austin replied. "Tell Tyler we're all in."

"Okay," she said, parting from them to go to her bus near the front of the line. "See you tomorrow."

She turned away and was almost to the bus when she saw Tyler coming from the other direction. She had finally learned why he was so late getting on the bus last Friday. After math this afternoon, he asked her to save

146

him a seat. His study period had to meet in one of the portables furthest from the busses on Fridays because their regular classroom was used as an advisors' meeting room. She'd told him she might not make it out much sooner than him because of wanting to check the cast list.

Brooke didn't ride the bus on Fridays because of her skating lessons, so she didn't know if they would find a seat together, but they did. She was prepared to tell him what Austin said about the band, but he spoke first.

"Did you get a part?"

She smiled. "Yes."

"One you wanted?"

"Yes," she laughed. "And one I'm not so sure about."

"What's that mean?"

She explained about being cast as an understudy as well, which she wouldn't be freaked out about if it wasn't for the lead role, but it was. She couldn't wrap her mind around that at this point.

"Are you serious?" he asked.

She nodded. "Crazy, huh?"

"Hmmm, not that crazy," he replied. "You must deserve it if they gave it to you."

She appreciated the compliment, but she wasn't sure *deserved* was the right word. "I guess I'm better at acting than I thought. I never feel like I'm doing very well, and I get really nervous, but it must look okay from out there."

"Are you nervous when you play keyboard at church?"

"Not really. I don't feel like all eyes are on me though. That's probably the difference. When you're speaking, everyone is looking at you."

"Is that why you don't want to sing in the band?"

"I don't like to be center-stage."

He didn't seem surprised by her admission, but he challenged her on it.

"You don't think anyone sees you up there playing keyboard?"

"No."

"You're very watchable, Emily."

She smiled. "To you maybe, but—"

"Not just to me. You have beautiful stage presence."

"I do?"

"Yes."

Her mom and dad told her that, but she thought they were saying so because they were her parents. "Can you keep a secret?"

"Sure."

"I—" She stopped, not wanting to say this unless he would swear to absolute secrecy. "Promise you won't tell anyone?"

"I promise."

"I've often wished I could be singing instead of playing keyboard."

"But no one has asked?"

"No. They know I can sing, but I play piano too, and no one else does, so that's been my place."

He smiled.

"You can't—"

"I won't," he assured her. "I'm just smiling because it's good to hear you admit you know you could do it."

~ CHAPTER SEVENTEEN ~

Brooke finished her warm-up exercises and saw her coach had arrived. Skating across the ice to where Elsa was waiting, she stopped along the wall and received her coach's standard greeting with a kiss on each cheek. Elsa was from Denmark, and she hadn't been living in the U.S. long, so her European customs and heavy accent were still very apparent.

"Hello, Brooke darling. How are you today?"

"Fine," she replied. "How are you?"

"Good, good. Sorry I am late. Let's get started. Competition is in one week. We can't waste a minute."

She had her work on her spins first, then her jumps, and then some of the finer details of her program. Designing a program was tedious, but Brooke liked how Elsa allowed her to be creative and let the music guide her steps, rather than dictating to her what she was going to do like some of her instructors in the past, and she was letting her do that even now, just a week before her competition next Saturday.

Beyond giving her guidance and direction, Elsa also gave her confidence. She pointed out her weaknesses freely but also helped her overcome them and was her greatest cheerleader.

After she had gone through her whole routine with the music, they were both confident she would be ready by next week, but they had some fine-tuning to do, so Elsa scheduled a couple of extra lesson times for next week.

"I think you're going to do wonderful at this competition, Brooke. Have you thought any more about moving up to the next level and increasing your regular practice schedule? I think you're more than ready for it."

"I've been thinking about it," she said. "I'll see how next Saturday goes."

Elsa smiled. "You're beautiful on the ice, darling. I'm sure you're going to do very well. You believe it too."

"Okay," she smiled. She wanted to believe it, and she felt good today. Hopefully she wouldn't get too nervous for the actual competition.

***

Sarah didn't expect Ryan to get her letter until Saturday, but he was on her mind all day Friday. She didn't regret her decision, but she wondered how they were going to do this, and how she was going to make it until tomorrow to hear from him.

After school she went to volleyball practice, and the activity got her mind off of him more than anything else had, but afterwards while she was walking out to meet whoever was picking her up today, there he was again, and she had half a mind to send him a text now, knowing he would respond by the time she got home.

Taking her phone out of her backpack, she turned it on, more to check for any messages than to actually contact Ryan. She had a text waiting from her mom saying she might be a few minutes late picking her up but she would try to be on time. Annalise had also texted her, asking if she wanted to come over to her house tonight after dinner to watch movies and have a sleepover. Sarah wasn't sure if she meant the two of them or if she was inviting a lot of girls, so she texted her back to ask.

Her mom wasn't there when she stepped outside, so she waited by the raised flowerbed area. Several of her teammates walked past to meet their rides as she was waiting, and they all said good-bye and wished her a good weekend. A couple of them asked if she was going to the football game tonight, and she told them no. It was an away game, and she had no desire to go.

Annalise texted back and said it would just be the two of them. Sarah knew she would have to ask but didn't see any reason why her parents would say no, so she replied and accepted the invitation, saying she would call her later about the exact time she could come. Just as she hit the send button, someone said her name, and she looked up to see a guy she had met this week. He was new and hadn't started until Monday. He was in several of her classes and had moved to Eugene from Hawaii. His dad had been in the Navy there but had gotten out at the end of August and they moved here to where his parents had grown up and his grandparents lived. He was nice and really cute, and they had talked several times this week.

"Hi, Kevin," she said. "Did you make the team?"

"Yeah, I did," he replied. He had been practicing with the soccer team this week and trying to earn a spot after the coach had already made the cuts two weeks ago.

"Congratulations!" she said. "That's great."

"Yeah, they're even putting me on JV."

"Wow, you must be better than you thought," she laughed.

"I guess so," he replied modestly. "How was your match yesterday?"

"Good. We won. I didn't play much, so I can't take credit for it, but I had fun."

"I wish I could have seen you play. Maybe next time."

She almost told him when their first home game was, but remembering Ryan, she decided against it. Kevin was nice, but she needed a best friend right now more than she needed a boyfriend. Her mom drove up, and she didn't hesitate to excuse herself, but she was nice about it.

"My ride is here," she said. "Have a nice weekend."

"You too, Sarah. Are you going to the game tonight?"

"No."

"Would you like to?"

She stopped and looked into his eyes. Over the last couple of years she had learned to read guys by looking in their eyes. And Kevin wasn't hard to read. His intentions were honest. He was just taking a chance and making a move, but she wasn't interested in starting something with anyone new right now. She and Ryan had unfinished business, and she couldn't wait to hear from him tomorrow.

"No, thanks," she replied. "I have plans. See you Monday."

He let her go, and she didn't look back. Getting into the car, she set her backpack at her feet and put on her seat-belt. She didn't breathe until her mom pulled out of the school entrance, and then she took a deep breath and let it out slowly.

"Everything all right?" she asked.

"Fine," she replied. "I'm glad it's Friday. Annalise asked if I could come over this evening and spend the night. Would that be all right?"

"Sure. Sometime later, or now?"

"Later. After dinner."

Her cell phone rang, and she reached into her bag. Taking it out, she looked at the display and smiled. It was Ryan. She debated about answering it with her mom in the car, but if she didn't, her mom would probably ask why, so she went ahead and took the call.

"Hi, Ryan."

"Hey," he replied.

She wondered if he had gotten the letter today, but she didn't have to ask. He gave it away.

"I love you, Sarah."

She smiled and felt tears stinging her eyes. Ryan was so sweet. So caring and transparent. He had never hidden his feelings from her.

"You got my letter," she replied. "I thought you wouldn't until tomorrow."

"I got it. When I didn't hear from you all week, I thought—. I'm glad you're not mad. Where are you?"

"In the car. I just got done with practice."

"Who's driving?"

"My mom."

"Can you ask if I can come see you next weekend?"

"Can you?"

"Yes. I already talked to my dad, and he said I can take the bus."

She hadn't thought that far ahead. "I haven't talked to them about this yet. Can I call you later?"

"Yes. We're going to the football game tonight, but we'll be home until six-thirty."

"I'm going to spend the night at a friend's house, so I'll call you before that."

"Do you still feel the same as when you wrote this letter, or are you having second-thoughts?"

"No second-thoughts," she assured him. "I know I need this. I've felt really at peace these last couple of days."

"I've only had an hour to let it sink in, but I haven't stopped smiling. I've missed you so much."

"I've missed you too."

"Okay, I'll let you go. Promise you'll call me?"

"Yes, I promise."

She hung up and glanced at her mom to see how much of that she had heard. She had every intention of telling her mom and dad about her decision, but she had wanted to wait until after she talked to Ryan and heard him say he wanted this too.

"Was that Ryan, Ryan? Or someone you've met here?"

"That was Ryan," she replied, not hiding a smile coming from the sweet feeling in her heart.

Her mom waited for her to elaborate, and she told her the basics, including that Ryan wanted to take the bus to see her next weekend. Her mom had pulled the car into the garage by the time she got to that detail, and she waited to hear her mom's reaction.

"Your dad and I have always liked Ryan," she said, smiling at her.

"So it's okay if he comes next Saturday?"

"I don't see why not. If it's okay with his parents."

She smiled and gave her mom a hug. Her mom didn't usually initiate hugs, but Sarah had learned she could do so, and hugging her mom always gave her a secure feeling.

After going inside and having some dinner her mom had cooking in the Crock-Pot all afternoon while she had been doing volunteer work at a health clinic, she called Annalise to let her know she could come over, and they decided on a time. She went upstairs to pack and then called Ryan from her phone. He was happy to hear it was okay for him to come down next weekend, and she said he could call her tomorrow afternoon and they could talk longer.

"I've missed talking to you," he said.

"I've missed talking to you too," she replied, and then added. "Actually, I've just missed you. Talking and everything else."

"Me too, Sarah. And I want you to know I don't have any certain expectations. I just—well, you know. I said it all already."

"I know, Ryan. And I like what you said. It made me realize I've been feeling the same way."

~ CHAPTER EIGHTEEN ~

The doorbell rang, and Emily went to answer it. Tyler was coming over for dinner, and he was right on time. Opening the door, she saw him standing there like she expected, but his appearance was surprising. He had dressed up, and he had flowers.

Holding them out to her, he didn't seem nervous. She took the flowers from him and said 'thank you'. He stepped inside and kissed her on the cheek. He had put on some cologne too, and he smelled nice.

"You dressed up," she said.

"It's our first date," he replied as if that was a perfectly good response, and she supposed it was. She hadn't really dressed up, but she had changed into something different than she'd been wearing at school.

She led the way to the kitchen, and he followed her. Her mom was getting dinner on the table, and she found a vase for the flowers. Her mom told her to put them on the table as a centerpiece, and she did. Her dad had come in to talk with Tyler, and she was listening to their conversation but not looking at them directly. She felt nervous about Tyler being here, and she wondered what this evening would hold. She hoped her parents wouldn't say anything embarrassing or make Tyler feel uncomfortable.

He sat beside her at dinner, and while her dad prayed before they ate, he held her hand. Tyler seemed relaxed and was being himself, but he was also well-mannered and respectful toward her parents. Her mom and dad asked Tyler lots of questions, and Emily learned some things about him. She already knew what his parents did for a living and that he had two younger sisters. Tatiana was eight, and Tasha was five. They were both attending the elementary school where Erin went, and Tyler was responsible for watching them when they got home from school, although his mom was home by four o'clock, so it was only for a half-hour.

She also knew Tyler didn't play football or soccer but he liked basketball and baseball and planned to try out for the school teams. And she knew he played trumpet, piano, and drums, but she learned he knew how to scuba dive, sail a boat, and he loved kayaking. Living by the ocean for so many years at the wide mouth of the Columbia River, all three of those made sense, but he hadn't shared those interests and hobbies with her yet.

"Does your dad do those things?" her dad asked.

"Yes, my mom too. They actually met on a kayak trip, and on their honeymoon they went scuba diving and sailing off the coast of Hawaii. My mom hadn't done either before, but my dad taught her."

Emily tried to imagine her own parents doing any of those things, but she couldn't. They liked to play golf, and their whole family went bike-riding sometimes, but otherwise they were more of an indoor family. Board games, family music sessions, and everyone sitting around reading were more their speed.

"Are your mom and dad musical too?" she asked, wondering if that's why he was.

"A little," he replied. "My mom played the piano when she was young, so she had me start taking lessons, but the other stuff I did on my own."

There was a slight pause in the conversation, and Tyler used the opportunity to ask her parents a question. "How did you meet, Mr. and Mrs. Hawthorne?"

Her mom let her dad answer. "We met in college," he said. "At the University of Oregon. We were both in choir, and we went to the same church. I asked her out one Sunday during our junior year, and we dated for a year and a half and got married the summer we graduated."

Emily knew there was more to the story, but she wasn't surprised her dad didn't elaborate. It was too personal to share with their fourteen year old daughter's boyfriend who was having dinner with them for the first time. Emily thought she might tell him sometime, but when it was just the two of them, and probably not for awhile.

After dinner Emily helped her mom with clearing the table, but her sisters were asked to help with the dishes, so Emily stepped back into the dining room to sit beside Tyler who was talking to her dad. Daddy excused himself after a few minutes, and once it was just the two of them, Tyler asked what she wanted to do. He was planning to be here until eight-thirty, and it was only six forty-five now.

"Would you like to see our music room?" she asked.

"Sure. Where is it?"

"Downstairs," she replied.

She led the way and opened the door that led to the basement. Turning on the light, she went first, and once they were at the bottom, they were there, although she had to turn on the main lights to see it. They had their nice keyboard set up along with a drum set, guitars, bongo drums, a xylophone, a hammered dulcimer, amps, monitors, speakers, and microphones.

"Whoa," he said. "When you said music room, you weren't kidding."

"We're a musical family," she replied. So used to seeing all of it, she knew she took it for granted, but she didn't know anyone else who had anything close to this.

He tried out the keyboard and appeared to appreciate its finer sound most people wouldn't notice. It was the first time she had ever heard him play, and he was very good. She wasn't surprised, but it seemed unreal he could actually play chords and make a full sound, not just plunk out *Mary Had A Little Lamb* or *Chopsticks* like a lot of her friends did.

"Did you write that?" she asked after he played a particular melody she didn't recognize but was very beautiful.

"Yes," he said. "No words though. Just the music."

"I write words," she reminded him.

"I know. I'd have us work on something now, but I'm still a little tired. Maybe next time."

"I'd like that."

After he had toured the room and tried out the other instruments, they went back upstairs, and she asked if he wanted dessert. He said yes, and she told him to sit in the formal living room and she would bring him some. Going to the kitchen, she dished up vanilla ice cream over a brownie and drizzled chocolate syrup on top. Taking two bowls into the living room where they weren't normally allowed to have food, she handed him his and sat beside him.

"I hope you like vanilla ice cream and brownies," she said. "I guess I should have asked."

"I like any dessert," he said. "Except cheesecake. I hate cheesecake."

"I'll remember that," she laughed. "Actually I don't like it much either. Or anything with lemon."

They ate in silence for a few moments, and Emily feared they had run out of things to talk about, but when Tyler finally spoke again, she realized he had been thinking about something.

"You know how you asked me earlier if my mom and dad are musical?"

"Yeah."

"Well, the man I call my dad isn't, but my real dad is."

"Real dad?"

"I never knew him. My mom dated him in high school, and after she got pregnant with me, he joined the Army, and she hasn't seen him since."

"I'm sorry," she said.

"It's okay. I didn't know my dad until I was five, but he's the dad I know, and he's been good to me and my mom. I'm sure it's better this way."

"How old was your mom when she had you?"

"Sixteen. He was a senior, but she was only a sophomore when they were together."

Emily was most surprised his mom had kept him rather than having an abortion or giving him up for adoption because she'd been so young, but she wasn't sure how to say that, so she asked him something.

"What instrument did your dad play?"

"Saxophone, drums, and piano. He was into jazz music mostly. That's how they met—in jazz band. My mom was the piano player. He played the sax."

"Did your mom finish high school?"

"Yes, eventually. She took a year off when she had me and then went back. My grandma took care of me while she did two years of community college too, and then my mom got married and got a job at a bank."

Emily had been feeling nervous about talking to Tyler about their relationship, how she wanted to take things slow and some other conditions of them spending time together, but now she supposed Tyler would understand them better than other guys at this age. Him dressing up tonight, talking to her parents the way he did, agreeing to spend time with her family rather than going out somewhere: it all suddenly made sense.

"Has your mom been telling you how to impress a girl and her parents?"

He smiled. "You could say that. Although, *impress* isn't the right word. Respect is better. 'If you want others to respect you, Tyler, you respect them.' She says that all the time."

Emily smiled.

"She wants to meet you. Do you think your mom and dad would let you come over to my house for dinner sometime?"

"If you ask them."

"I'll do that," he said but didn't get up right then.

She decided to do something before she changed her mind. Setting her half-eaten bowl of dessert on the coffee table, she excused herself and said she would be right back. Going up to her room, she grabbed the list from where she had tucked it inside her journal.

"What's that?" he asked as she set it facedown on the table and picked up her dessert to finish it before the ice cream melted.

"Just some things I want to talk about," she replied.

He took the last bite of his dessert and set the bowl on the table. Leaning back against the couch, he closed his eyes for a few moments, and she remembered him saying he felt tired. Once she had finished with her brownie, she took both of their bowls to the kitchen and then returned. His eyes were still closed, but when she sat down, he opened them.

She smiled, and he smiled in return. Reaching for her hand, he held it gently.

"Have you ever done this before, Tyler?"

"What?"

"Had a girlfriend? You seem well-versed in the rituals of modern courtship."

He laughed. "I'm not sure why you're making this so easy, but you are, Emily. I've never done this before. I didn't even have any friends who were girls back in Astoria."

She laughed.

He pointed to the piece of paper lying on the table. "So, what do you want to talk about?"

She reached for it. Looking at the list, she knew each point was important, and she decided to go for it.

Maybe he would laugh or not want to talk about this stuff, but if what she had seen from him tonight was any indication, she doubted it.

~ CHAPTER NINETEEN ~

Emily went down her list, one condition at a time, and Tyler was agreeable to everything she wanted, even the one about him coming to church on a regular basis with her family. She asked him if he believed in God, and he said he did. He hadn't been taught about Him in a formal way by attending church like she had since she was a little girl, but his mom had always told him to say his prayers and believe in miracles, and he saw the man who had married his mom and adopted him as his son as an answer to those prayers he whispered as a little boy.

"What else have you prayed for?" she asked.

"Not much that I remember until Tasha was born and she got sick when she was three months old. I was only nine, but I remember my mom being scared, and after my dad brought me and Tatiana home from the hospital to get some sleep but my mom stayed with Tasha, I just asked God to make her better, and then a couple of days later she was fine."

Emily couldn't think of anything she had prayed for that was as huge as asking God for a parent or to heal one of her sisters. Her requests, and sometimes demands, were much more petty: A nice keyboard she could have in her room when they already had a beautiful piano in the living room and a top-of-the-line keyboard in the basement; A cat, which they couldn't have because Elise was allergic to them; For Austin to stop liking Sarah, and then Brianne, so he could be her boyfriend instead.

"I asked him for something else too," Tyler said.

"What?"

"That we wouldn't have to move here."

She could see how that would be a big deal to him and wasn't surprised he had prayed for such a thing, just as she had prayed she wouldn't have to go to public high school.

"Does that mean you've lost faith?" she asked, sort of teasing him, but also wondering if he was mad at God for not keeping his family in Astoria.

He smiled and looked at her directly with his expressive green eyes. They looked different in this light than on the school bus. They glistened.

"Maybe for a few weeks, but I needed to be more patient and see what He had waiting for me here."

She didn't know what to say. Had God brought him here to meet her? Was Tyler an answer to all the prayers she had prayed about Austin, only God had brought her someone who was more suited for her—a better answer than the one she wanted for herself?

His eyes moved to her lips, and she knew he was thinking about kissing her. And she wanted him to, but that was the last thing on her list—asking him to hold off on that for now until she knew she wanted him to be her first kiss. And she didn't think she could know that yet.

Biting her lower lip, she lowered her eyes and spoke before she waited too long and didn't have a chance to share her wishes on that. "I have one more thing on my list," she said, lifting her eyes once again.

He was still looking at her. "What?"

She held up the paper, and he glanced away. Pointing to the last phrase, she let him read it for himself. He smiled before he looked back at her, and she felt her sweetest smile emerge.

"Sorry," she whispered.

"Don't be. I can wait."

They were both quiet for a moment, and then he said something else.

"Can I see some of your songs?"

"Right now?"

"Unless you had other plans."

"No," she replied. "I'll get my notebook. It's in my room."

She left his side and went upstairs again. She had more than one song notebook, but she took the one from her desk with her most recent scribblings of lyrics. Recently she had gone through them and circled her favorites, but she had written several pages since then. One thing about facing the crisis of going to public school: it had released a lot of emotions she couldn't hold inside. Writing a song was great for her troubled soul.

She felt nervous about showing Tyler tender words from her heart, fearing he would think they were dumb or not very good. She didn't think he would actually say so. He was too nice to be rude or laugh. But she worried he would secretly think she was wasting her time, and she wanted him to be honest, but she didn't know if she could take it.

Still, after so many years of keeping them to herself, not even showing her family, returning to Tyler's side to let him take a look gave her a nervous thrill. He looked tired, however, and she said they didn't have to do this right now if he wanted to rest or go home early.

"Go home?" he laughed. "I've been waiting all week to be here. I'm not going home an hour early."

She smiled, keeping the purple notebook closed for the moment. In a way she wanted Tyler to snatch it from her and start reading, but he didn't.

"Are these all the songs you've ever written?" he asked.

"No, just in the last year or so. I wrote a lot when I was younger but hadn't for awhile, and then one day I was shopping with my mom for school supplies and saw this purple notebook and decided to get it and start writing again."

"You like purple," he noted.

"Yes. How did you guess?"

"I like purple too," he said. "Not as much as you, but I like it."

"What is your favorite color?"

"Red."

She could have guessed that. He had a red backpack and often wore a red hoodie to and from school, but he reminded her of another shade of red he liked by looking at her—or more specifically her hair. She smiled and felt beautiful, something she didn't experience often.

"Okay, enough stalling," he said. "Show me your songs."

She opened the front cover. Flipping through several pages, she looked for one that was circled and stopped to scan the title and first verse. It was decent, and she moved her hand out of the way so he could read the words, but he had a different idea.

"Read it to me," he said, turning more to face her. "I'm better with hearing poetry than reading it."

She agreed and began reading the words to him. She didn't think she had ever read them out loud before, but the rhyme and rhythm was good, and she didn't think the words sounded too dorky. Maybe a little blah and cliché in some places, but not bad.

Tyler had an interesting look on his face when she finished. She waited for him to say something. He let out a whoosh of air and summed up his initial reaction in one word.

"Wow."

She smiled.

"That was amazing," he said, taking the notebook from her and reading the words himself. After scanning the page for a few moments, he handed it back to her. "You're good, Emily. Better than I thought you'd be. Not that I didn't think you could write, but I was trying to keep in mind you're only fourteen."

She didn't say anything. His words meant a lot to her. And she liked the idea of being good at something she enjoyed so much. She liked acting and singing and playing piano. Keyboarding for the worship band was probably her favorite thing to do of those talents, but writing songs came from a different place within her, and she always enjoyed putting her thoughts down and stringing words and phrases together.

In some ways it came naturally, but she also had to work at it, and she usually felt good after writing something, even if the words came from pain and heartache.

"I like that one," she said.

"Read me more."

She turned a few pages and found another circled one. Going ahead with it, she read the whole thing. She thought it was better than the first in terms of the quality of writing, but she wasn't sure how someone would compare them in a subjective way. Tyler gave his opinion.

"I like that one even better."

He had his eyes closed, and she looked through some more without reading any until she came to one she really liked. In addition to being circled, the words also had stars around them.

"Are you still awake?" she whispered.

He opened his eyes and smiled. "Yes, go ahead."

She read it all the way through. It was more of a story than the other two, and it was a true story about her life. From her childhood to something that happened this past year that taught her a profound truth about herself. She was often reaching for things that were out of reach, but in time those things became attainable and even sweeter because she'd had to wait for them.

She didn't feel like reading any more after that, and she honestly didn't care if Tyler liked it more or less than the others. The words meant something to her personally, even if they never became a song anyone heard. Tyler had been watching her the whole time, and when she closed the notebook, he reached out and took her hand thoughtfully.

"You have to promise me something, Emily."

"What?"

"You'll let me write music for you and share these with the band."

"If you think they're good enough."

"They're good enough, and hopefully I can write the music to do them justice."

Her thoughts returned to something he said earlier. "I liked what you said about God answering your prayer in a better way than you asked for. I'm starting to feel the same way about not being homeschooled anymore. I couldn't imagine anything good coming out of that, but now I can see He knew things I didn't."

She felt too overwhelmed by her current circumstances to say anything else. To have Tyler here sitting in her living room was amazing enough, something she never would have imagined happening two weeks ago when she started her first day of public high school. But it wasn't just Tyler. She liked school. She liked seeing her friends every day. She liked her less busy schedule. She had a part in the school play, and she was talking to someone who liked her lyrics and wanted to make songs out of them.

And she was only two weeks into her freshman year. What was next? What other sweet surprises awaited her? As if she even needed a next thing. This was more than enough.

They were interrupted by her dad coming into the room to see what they were up to. She felt embarrassed he caught Tyler holding her hand, but her thoughts were too consumed with other realities to care much.

"Hi, Dad," she said, responding to him clearing his throat to announce his presence.

"Hey, kiddo," he said. "Did you two want dessert?"

"We already had some, thanks."

"Okay. I was checking to see if you two are all right in here."

"We're fine," she replied.

He checked his watch. "It looks like you have about thirty minutes left. Or did you need to get out of here sooner, Tyler?"

"No, I'm good," Tyler said. "I'll take the full thirty minutes, Sir."

"We're just in the family room if you need anything."

Emily almost laughed, but she managed to hold it in. She wasn't sure who was more dorky, her dad or herself. Fortunately Tyler was gracious to both of them.

"Thank you, Sir. I think we'll be right here. Emily was sharing some of her songs with me. I'd like to help her write music for them. Could we use the music room next time for that?"

"S-Sure," he said. He didn't say he didn't know she wrote songs, but Emily knew that's what he was thinking. "I hear you're thinking of starting a band."

"Yes. Me and Austin and some of the other guys. We want Emily and Brianne to be a part of it too, and—what's the other girl's name?"

"Marissa," she said.

"That sounds like a good crew," her dad replied.

Emily could see him getting ready to launch into a big speech about how to run a band and staying true to

172

the message in the music, but this wasn't the time, and she gave him a look.

He stopped himself. "Well, as you were."

She thanked him with a smile, and he left. Tyler didn't seem bothered by the intrusion, and he was excited her dad had agreed to let them use the music room. He leaned over and kissed her cheek.

"Do you think they'll let me come back tomorrow?"

"You can ask."

"Do you want me to?"

"Yes," she said. "I like you being here. I like you, Tyler."

"I like you too, Emily. Very much."

~ CHAPTER TWENTY ~

Having Austin over at her house on Friday night was a different experience for Brianne than being at his. Hers was much more noisy and filled with activity at every turn. They never had more than five minutes alone, but she was having fun, and Austin seemed fine with being here also.

Brianne wondered how Emily's time with Tyler was going tonight. Emily had seemed shy about it when she told her of their plans during choir this afternoon, but Brianne was excited for her, and happy Emily felt comfortable telling her. Tyler had told Austin too, and Austin didn't have any reason to believe Tyler's interest in Emily wasn't genuine and something that could be a good thing for both of them.

"How do you think Tyler will feel about Emily's conditions?" she asked while they were waiting at the table for everyone to come join them for a game.

"That depends on what his motive is," he replied.

"What do you mean?"

"If he's interested in friendship, getting to know Emily, and having time with her, he'll be fine with waiting for other things; but if he's looking to have a girlfriend and getting what he wants out of it, then he'll either try to talk her into what he wants, or move on to someone else."

Brianne recalled a time she had gone to the movies with Sarah before their seventh grade year, shortly before Sarah moved away. They ran into two guys at the theater. One of them was Brady, and he liked Sarah and was trying to get her to go out with him. The other one was Danny. She knew both of them from school, and while Brady was talking to Sarah and trying to convince her to be his girlfriend, he tried to set up a double date, placing her with Danny.

Sometimes she wondered what would have happened if Sarah had accepted the invitation and drug her into it too. Not that she thought Sarah had been tempted to, because Sarah wasn't interested, but if she had been a different friend who was waiting for a guy like Brady to notice her. Brianne was convinced after watching Brady and Danny at school over the last couple of years that neither of them had pure intentions when it came to girls, and going out with either one of them would not have been a good experience.

She shuddered to think about it and gained a new appreciation for Austin. He hadn't only been a great friend to her who always treated her well and respected her wishes regarding what kind of friends they were, but he had also protected her from getting involved with other guys who may not have been so agreeable to her desire for friendship above anything else.

"Why are you looking at me like that?" he asked, taking the game board out of the box and setting it flat on the table.

They didn't have the privacy here for her to say much, so she kept it simple. "I appreciate you, Austin. That's all."

"You better," he replied.

She laughed.

He smiled also, and even though he was teasing her, she knew he wanted to be the kind of friend to her he was. If he didn't, he wouldn't be here tonight and hang out with her every day at school.

She and Austin were teamed up together for the game with Beth, and they won. It was after eight by the time they finished, and Brianne assumed Austin wouldn't stay much longer. It was too late to start a family movie, but her younger siblings would be up for a little while longer before it was their bedtime, so it wasn't like they could start one of their own, and by the time they were all in bed and the living room was free, it would be too late.

But he did stay to play a video game with her brothers, and since J.T.'s bedtime wasn't until nine-thirty, her mom and dad didn't say anything about them needing to stop when it was time for Jeffrey and Steven to get ready for bed. She had helped Beth take a bath and wash her hair, and seeing Austin was still occupied with the game, she read to Beth before her mom came to tuck her in.

Going back to the living room, she smiled when she saw him. "Are you still here?"

"What? You stay later than this at my house."

"I know," she replied. "But your house isn't this crazy."

"This isn't crazy," he said. "It's never boring."

"That's true," she replied, recalling her mother's words she often used whenever she said she was bored. 'I can find something for you to do.'

For now she chose to enjoy the fact she didn't have anything to do except sit and watch Austin and her brother playing, even if it was a game she didn't understand. She really liked it when Austin spent time with J.T. because her younger brother looked up to him, and Austin was the most positive role model in his life close to his age.

She could have kissed him earlier when J.T. asked Austin if he wanted Tyler to start playing drums for worship band instead of him, and Austin hadn't hesitated to reply: "No way, man. That's your place as long as you want it to be."

But she wasn't planning to kiss Austin anytime soon, and she wanted to keep it that way, even if there were times he was completely irresistible. Her decision to not have a boyfriend right now was still firm, and she had several reasons for keeping it that way, but one of them had resurfaced this afternoon when she read an email from Sarah.

Hearing Sarah was going to be returning to her relationship with Ryan, possibly in a boyfriend-girlfriend kind of way, had reminded her things could change very quickly. A week ago she considered Joel off-limits because Sarah had admitted to liking him, and she had no desire to get in the way of them getting together if that's what they both wanted. But if Sarah was choosing Ryan, that left the possibility open for her to have something beyond friendship with Joel once again. Not right now, but perhaps in the future.

Before she went to bed, she took the letters she had received from Joel over the last few years and looked through them. Something he said in one of them had been on her mind this evening, and she wanted to read his exact words again. She knew exactly when he had written it—after they spent time together at camp two summers ago between her seventh and eighth grade year. She had spent a few days with Sarah, Austin, and Joel but had some time alone with Joel shortly before they left.

On their walk around the lake, Joel admitted he didn't want her to leave because he was going to miss her, and also because he knew she was going home with Austin and he was afraid of "losing" her to him. It had surprised her because Joel had never said anything like that to her before, but she'd been having a desire for him to kiss her, so he wasn't the only one thinking that way.

They had parted well, however, and she wrote him a letter restating the things she shared with him face to face about not going there with each other yet, but keeping the option open for the future, and he had written back, saying he agreed and sharing more of his thoughts with her she had never forgotten to this day.

I have a confession to make. I almost kissed you on Friday when we went for that walk. On Thursday night I heard God saying, 'You have to let her go, Joel. You can't try and hang on to her right now', but I didn't want to listen. I thought, 'If I kiss her now, then I won't have to let her go. She'll be mine, not Austin's. She'll be going home with him, but I'll have her heart.'

But now I'm really glad I didn't because I know that's not fair to you. I shouldn't be making you choose between us right now or ever. That's your decision to make at the right time for you. And not just with me and Austin but with anyone. Don't let any guy kiss you until you're ready, Brianne. Not even me! Don't let go of God's best for you. Not now or when we're sixteen. I know you won't let me do that, and I won't let you either—even if it means letting go of you then too.

She sighed every time she read those words, but it had been awhile, so they hit her more deeply than ever, especially in light of her current circumstances. After letting go of Joel in her heart several months ago when she learned of Sarah and Joel's mutual interest in one another, it felt strange to have him "back". But it was a pleasant thought. Austin was her best friend here, but Joel was one of her best friends in a different way, and at this point she couldn't predict the future. She wanted to, but she couldn't, and she knew that was a good thing. A difficult thing, but good.

She wondered if Sarah would write Joel and tell him about her renewed feelings for Ryan, and how he would feel about it, but she wasn't going to be the one to say anything. They had plans to go visit his family at Thanksgiving, and she didn't anticipate having any time with him before then. She thought about writing a letter to him just to say 'hi', but she decided to wait a few days and see if he was still on her mind and how she was feeling at that point.

She had a familiar anxiousness to grow up and be at a place in life where she could make definite decisions about these kinds of things, but she didn't want to go beyond being fourteen because she wasn't, and for the most part her life was uncomplicated.

The following afternoon, however, she was reminded her life often became complicated overnight. She received Sarah's handwritten letter in the mail, along with one from David who hadn't written to her since sending her some of his song lyrics after meeting him at camp this summer.

He sent her more he had written in the last month, and he also enclosed a personal letter. It was handwritten rather than typed as his previous letter had been, and she noticed he had really nice penmanship for a guy, and something about seeing his handwriting made her feel a deeper connection to him.

Dear Brianne,

Hi. Thanks for your letter. I'm glad you've had a chance to look at my songs and don't think they're completely worthless. I appreciate your kind words and encouragement. I'm sending you some I've written since camp, but don't feel obligated to comment on them or show them to Austin if you're already working on others. I just felt like sharing these with you, and I hope they touch your heart if nothing else.

I've been thinking about you a lot, Brianne. More than I probably should, but I can't help it. I thought it was because I didn't have much to think about until school got started, but the last two weeks have been more of the same. Only now I see you around every corner at school. I'll be thinking about the class I came from or the one I'm going to, and then all of the sudden I see a girl with a similar hairstyle or a beautiful smile like you, and for a moment I actually see you. Not in a "going-crazy" way, but as a nice reminder, and then I spend the next ten minutes thinking about you instead of concentrating in class.

I think it would help if you wrote me back and said, 'Leave me alone. Not interested.' I'd completely understand and be content with keeping this strictly about my songs, or not even that if I'm creeping you out by saying this stuff. I don't do this, Brianne. I don't share my songs with pretty girls or pour my heart out. And I don't say that to get your pity and make you feel like you can't reject me. I say that because it's true.

Anyway, I've been thinking about something, and I'll go ahead and tell you so it doesn't keep swimming around in my head every day. I go to a lot of concerts. It's my favorite thing to do besides write songs, and I always come away feeling inspired to write more— maybe that's my problem, I go to concerts that fill my head with crazy dreams of being a famous songwriter—but anyway, I do, and I was thinking the next one I go to could be in Portland, and my reason would be to meet you there. You could invite Austin or any of your friends, or you could come by yourself, *or you don't have to meet me there at all. Honestly, Brianne. I'm not trying to talk you into something you have no interest in doing. I'm just looking for a way to see you again, and if you'd like to see me but have a better idea, I'm open to whatever suggestions you may have.*

Okay, I'm going to shut up now. I have no idea why I'm smiling. I should be beating my head against the wall and saying, 'You're an idiot, David.' But I'm not. I think that has to do with you, Brianne. You might reject me, but I know you'll at least be nice about it. I really do hope you like the songs. I often feel they have a mind and heart of their own, which makes sense if they're from a place beyond my own thoughts.

Which leads me to a question I will leave you with. What's your passion, Brianne? What are your "songs"? Is it singing or something else? Or are you still waiting to discover whatever it is? That's okay if you are, I'm just wondering.

Sincerely,
David

~ CHAPTER TWENTY-ONE ~

There's a love in my heart
That I can't explain
It grows deeper each day
And never grows dim

Where does it come from
And where does it go
Its flow has no ending
That's all I know

The heart of my God
Cannot be explained
With mere words and nice rhymes
It's felt and it's shown

From my heart to yours
From heaven and back
Like a fire in a hearth
Like a calm in the storm

This would be so much easier if David didn't write such great songs, Brianne thought, sighing and continuing to read the words on the pages David had sent her along with a letter professing his love for her, practically anyway.

Her one consolation was she didn't have to make an official decision about David right now. She could agree to meet him at a concert without it having to be a date. She could hide behind her, 'I'm not dating yet so don't ask' card, but still spend time with David as a friend. Her main concern with his admission and invitation was having to tell Austin about it, which she knew she had to do no matter what she decided. It was the one thing she found most difficult about having him for a best friend. She couldn't hide anything from him, and she didn't want to, but it wasn't always easy to tell him things related to other guys, even if he had been the one to encourage David to write to her in the first place!

She saw him an hour later at worship band practice, and she was thankful for the distraction of Emily and Tyler who seemed to have had a nice time together last night. They had spent part of this afternoon together before coming here, and Emily told them she wanted Tyler to learn some of their regular songs on keyboard so they could rotate from week to week on Sundays, rather than her being their sole keyboard player.

Austin had the additional idea of having Emily or Tyler play the regular piano on songs both instruments sounded good together on, and Brianne knew Tyler was doing something serious to Emily's heart if she was willing to share the stage with someone who was as equally talented as her—which Tyler obviously was.

Brianne never would have pegged him as a musician when she first met him, other than playing an instrument in the band, but he was very talented. More than she could ever hope to be if she practiced ten hours a day for ten years.

David's question about what her passion was came to mind several times, and she didn't know yet. She liked to sing, but she didn't see it as something she had to do all the time. She liked acting, she liked to play the flute, she liked to read, she liked to write letters, she liked a lot of things; but to define something she loved and was truly passionate about, nothing came to mind.

After their regular worship band practice, they took a little break and had pizza Austin's dad brought for them, and then they had their first "band" rehearsal that for now consisted of Austin, Tyler, Emily, Marissa, Michael, Trevor, and herself. Trevor was the bass player, and he was a senior this year, easily making him the oldest member of the group, but he seemed content with letting Austin and Tyler be the primary leaders as they all practiced familiar songs together and tried a couple of new ones Austin had gotten the music for online this week.

They weren't ready for practicing their own songs yet. Austin and Tyler needed to work on writing the music for all the instruments, but Tyler did play something on the keyboard for them he'd come up with this afternoon. It was more of a ballad, and Brianne wondered if it was something Emily had written before he said so. Emily's shy but non-embarrassed smile emerged when he bragged on her, and Brianne felt happy to see Emily being so herself with him, but it also made her think of

David and how much she was holding his heart in her hands in the same way right now.

She didn't have any plans to go to Austin's house after rehearsal, but his dad was taking her home on their way, and Austin asked her something in the truck when David was on her mind.

"You're being quiet tonight. Is everything okay?"

They were in the back seat of the double cab truck, but it didn't have enough privacy for her to talk about it. When she didn't respond, he knew something was up without her having to say so.

"Do you want to come over or tell me tomorrow?"

She smiled at the fact not telling him wasn't an option. And she would rather tell him now, but she didn't know if deciding to go to his house without asking her parents first would be okay. She decided to live with the lesser of her concerns, knowing if she called her mom and dad when she got there and they wanted her to be at home, they could always come get her, but she would still have enough time to tell Austin about David's proposal.

Her parents didn't have any objection to her being at the Lockhart's for however long she was welcome to stay. Her dad said to call when she needed a ride home. She knew with it being Saturday and them having church in the morning, it would be better for her to not stay too late, but there was no need to say what she had to say and then rush home.

After they had gotten leftover cake from his mom's birthday that had been this week, they went to Austin's room, and she told him everything in between bites of her dessert and sips of strawberry soda. Austin didn't say anything until after she went silent, and she knew what he was going to say, but she needed to hear him say it.

"You know it's fine if you want to go. With me or on your own. Have you told your mom and dad yet?"

"No," she laughed. "But I'd be fine if they say I can't go. In a way I hope they do."

"Do you want to go?"

"I don't know. Maybe. I don't think I want to go by myself though. I think it would be fun if we both went, but I'm not sure how David would like that. He said it was fine, but he doesn't know how close we are, and I feel like not telling him would be unfair."

"That's a good point," Austin agreed. "Glad I'm not you."

She laughed at his teasing. "You're the one who got me into this!"

"No, no, no," he argued. "That was all you, Brianne. You stole his heart. I had nothing to do with it."

"Exactly! If you would have said something, I wouldn't be in this position."

"And what was I supposed to say?"

She didn't know. She knew what she wished he had said, but telling David she was his girlfriend wasn't truthful, so he couldn't.

"How can dating be so complicated when I'm not even dating yet?"

He smiled. "Just growing up is complicated. Nobody said being a teenager is easy, no matter how hard you try."

She had been thinking of something while Tyler was playing Emily's song, and she knew it was her best option if she could convince David to agree to it, and it would also be the most legitimate reason for her to see him again without any false pretenses.

"I was thinking of asking him to come here instead. Like spend Friday night here with you and then I could come over on Saturday and we could work on songs together. What do you think?"

"You want your boyfriend to spend the night at my house! There are limits to our friendship, Brianne."

She laughed but didn't believe his words for a second. "There are not. You've told me so."

"Yeah, okay. And I don't think you'll have to do much convincing. If it involves you and music—no problem."

She didn't know if she should be more upfront about defining her relationship with Austin before seeing David again, but for now her mind went a different direction.

"What's your passion, Austin?"

He lifted his eyes from the guitar he had picked up and got an interesting expression on his face. "My what?"

"Your passion. The thing you love more than anything. Like David and his songs. He asked me that, and I don't know what mine is yet. Do you?"

He looked at her and smiled. "I know."

She waited for him to go on, expecting him to say playing guitar, writing songs, or leading worship. A year ago she would have expected him to say skateboarding, and although he still liked to do that, she knew music had taken over his heart in a way skating never could.

But he didn't say any of those things. He remained silent.

"Well," she laughed. "What is it?"

"It's not an it," he replied.

She didn't follow, nor did she recognize the song he began to play. She recognized it in terms of knowing she had heard the chord progression and rhythm before, but she couldn't place the words.

"Are you going to tell me?" she asked over the sound of the guitar.

"I know what yours is," he said, stopping his strumming for a moment.

"You do?"

"Yep."

"What?"

"Your friends."

She thought about that and could see what he meant. She had a very strong desire to not only have friends, but to be a friend, even to those who were difficult to get along with or frustrated her by the choices they made. Sometimes she felt like it was a curse because she couldn't stop caring about them, even when they pushed her away or said hurtful things, but in the end she always knew it benefitted her to show them love instead of staying mad or giving up.

"So, what's yours?" she asked again. "Besides knowing me better than I know myself."

He kept playing without responding, but eventually he added the words of the familiar music when he got to the chorus, and then she recognized the song in an instant.

Only you
Is who I want
Only you, is who I've got
To hold my hand and walk this path

191

That I'm scared to tread
All by myself
Only you

It was the song he had written for her this summer, and while it touched her heart the first time she read the words and when he sang it for her a few weeks later, she took them into her heart more now in light of their current conversation.

"I'm your passion?" she said softly as he continued to strum his guitar. "Is that what you're saying?"

"That's what I'm saying, Brianne. It's like you are with your friends. Only for me, I feel that way about you. If you're happy, I'm happy. And if you're not, I want to do whatever I can to make you smile again."

~ CHAPTER TWENTY-TWO ~

Austin kept playing the music of the song, and Brianne listened. When he stopped, she asked him to sing the whole thing for her, but he claimed he didn't know all the words by heart.

She knew which notebook they were in because he let her read the words on their way home from camp. Seeing the blue cover in his stack of music, she reached for the composition book and found the page, remembering it was toward the middle because she realized how many songs he had been writing over the summer.

"Here you go," she said, laying the notebook on the bed where he was sitting and then going back to her chair.

He sighed. She was being a pest, but he started from the beginning, singing all of the words this time. He didn't have the timing down perfectly on some of the phrases because he hadn't practiced it enough, but she didn't care. She was interested in hearing the words again and allowing them to penetrate her heart.

When he finished, he held the guitar on his knee for a few seconds but then put it away on its stand at the end of his bed, acting as though that had drained him—

pouring out his heart to her yet again but knowing he couldn't act on his feelings for her yet, if ever.

She wasn't sure what she wanted to say to him, but she knew she wanted to say something. Slowly rising from the chair, she crossed the space between them and sat beside him on the bed, something she had never done before in this room. He didn't react to her sudden closeness, but her heart was pounding, and she felt like crying.

Austin's calmness confused her. She had no idea what she was doing, or if she should be doing it, but she either had to pretend Austin's declaration of love meant nothing to her, or she had to tell him what she was feeling. There was no in between.

She did the safest thing she could think of, giving him a hug and letting the tears fall. He didn't resist and held her close. She knew there were a million things she could say, but she said the one foremost on her mind.

"I don't deserve you, Austin."

He released her and sat back, appearing baffled by her words. "What?"

She couldn't look at him and dropped her eyes. "I don't. You're so good to me, and I'm—. I'm sorry."

"Sorry? For what?"

"For being so—" She wasn't sure what the right word was. He tried to help.

"So beautiful...amazing...encouraging...?"

She knew he was trying to make her laugh and prove a point, but she wasn't going to let him. Not this time. "So impossible!"

She was being completely serious, but he laughed. "You're not impossible, Brianne."

He was looking at her. Those light blue eyes were familiar from a distance but not close up. She should be this close more. Why wouldn't she let it happen?

"Why me, Austin?" she whispered. "Why am I your passion? Why not music or skateboarding or writing songs?"

"Those are just things, Brianne. You're the one I live for."

She closed her eyes. He was proving her point. He was completely willing to give her his heart, and she was being impossible about letting him. She felt sick of herself and tried to get up and leave, but he wouldn't let her.

Grabbing her elbow, he drew her back to him gently and gave her a hug. She resisted at first but slowly relaxed in his arms.

"I say that, Brianne, because you're worth living for. You're worth waiting for. You are beautiful and amazing and I love you for exactly who you are. If I could change anything about you, I wouldn't. I only want you to be you."

She admitted something to him. "You could kiss me right now and I wouldn't object."

He leaned back and looked into her eyes. Smiling briefly, he kissed her on the forehead and let out a laughing sigh. "Sorry, baby. Not today."

***

When Emily returned home after practice with the band, she went to her room to do homework. She had gotten a little done this morning before Tyler came to work on music, but she still had all of her assignment in science to do, and she also needed to write a short essay for her literature class.

The work itself wasn't difficult for her, but she had a tough time concentrating. One minute she was looking for an answer in her textbook, and the next she would catch herself daydreaming. Spending several hours with Tyler between last night and today had been surprisingly sweet. She had expected to have an okay time with him, but it hadn't been as awkward as she had feared, and he'd been so easy to talk to she couldn't quite believe it.

Last night had been nice with getting to know him better and having him agree to her conditions of them spending time together, but today had gone to a different level. Tyler was more talented musically than she had anticipated, and hearing him putting music to her song lyrics had been so fun and amazing. Everything he played sounded good. Some of it was beautiful, some was edgy, some was fun and lighthearted. And he loved to experiment. Nothing was set in stone. He wanted her to like it. He wanted to be happy with it. He wanted to play around and see how something sounded one way and then another. He reminded her of one of her favorite dance teachers in that way, only this wasn't about dancing to someone else's music. This was her music he was bringing to life, and it was a dream come true.

But it wasn't just the music, it was Tyler too. Everything about him was surprising. For only being fourteen, he had a mature quality to him. Like Austin, only Tyler was more reserved and didn't put himself out there for everyone to see. Although, she had known

Austin for a lot longer, so it was difficult to compare them.

Her mom interrupted when she was almost finished with her science questions. She wanted to know if she was hungry. They'd had pizza at the church, but that had been three hours ago, and she supposed she could use a snack. Her family had eaten tacos for dinner, and there were leftovers.

"Can I just have the fixings without the shell?" she asked.

"Sure. I'll bring a plate up for you."

"Thanks, Mom," she replied, feeling surprised she would let her eat in her room. For a long time all the house rules had been the same, but lately they had been changing. A later bedtime she'd expected, but others were more surprising. Her dad had asked Tyler if he wanted to come over for awhile this evening instead of taking him home right away liked they'd planned, but Tyler had a lot of homework to make up from being sick, so he had declined the offer. After having him here all afternoon, Emily was surprised her dad hadn't been more anxious to separate them.

When her mom returned with her taco salad and a glass of water, Emily thanked her and took a break. She had finished with science and needed time to think about what she wanted to write for her essay. Her mom didn't leave immediately and asked about her day. She was curious about how much time they had been downstairs in the music room.

"Your dad said every time he checked on you, you were working on something different."

"Tyler is really good," she said. "He can make music for anything."

"How many songs have you written?"

Emily pointed to her notebook on the bed next to where her mom was sitting. "Everything in there. And some other stuff I wrote when I was younger."

Her mom asked if she could look at them. Emily said it was fine, and she knew what was coming. The notebook was practically filled.

"Emily!" she said, turning from one page to the next. "Why haven't you ever shown us this?"

She shrugged. "I could never write any music for them, so I didn't see the point."

"Your dad can write music."

"I know, but he writes the lyrics and the music all at once. I couldn't do that."

"Why did you show these to Tyler?"

"He asked if I wrote songs, so I showed him."

Her mom smiled. "I guess I never thought to ask."

"It's just something I do in my spare time, which I had a lot more of this summer than ever before."

"We do get busy sometimes, don't we?" she sighed.

"I like not being so busy," she replied, hardly believing she was saying that, but it was true.

"How do you like school?"

"It's all right. Better than I thought it would be."

"Your dad and I talked it over, and it's fine if you want to accept Tyler's invitation for you to have dinner at his house sometime."

"Okay."

"He seems like a nice boy, Emily. Are you enjoying the time you've spent with him?"

"Yes. He's nice."

"Does he want us to pick him up for church tomorrow?"

"Yes. I think he likes going."

Her mom didn't say anything else on that subject and lowered her eyes to read the songs in her notebook. Emily knew spending time with a boy who didn't normally attend church was something for her mom to be concerned about because she had dated a guy in college who hadn't been a Christian and had no interest in church or God.

Her mom tried to get him to go to church with her for a long time, but he never would. Somehow she fell in love with him anyway, and ending the relationship had been a very difficult thing for her to do, and she may not have without her dad's help.

They had been friends at the time. Emily had heard the story, mostly from her grandmother's point of view. Whenever they went to her house in Newport for Thanksgiving, Christmas, or the Fourth of July, her grandma liked to bring up the subject at some point and praise her son-in-law for "coming to the rescue."

Her parents always agreed that was the case, but the last few times, Emily had noticed her mom seeming to only laugh out of politeness, and she realized her mom had tired of being reminded she almost made "the biggest mistake of her life."

When they were there this summer for the annual family reunion, they'd had to share about the changes taking place in the family with her dad's job in jeopardy and her mom going back to work. Her grandmother had her opinions on it all, mostly based on her own thoughts rather than the reality of their financial situation, but in the end she had conceded that even if her son-in-law was experiencing a "temporary setback" at least he had saved the day twenty years ago. Emily caught her mother crying in an out-of-the way place later, and she wondered if her tears had something to do with her grandmother's outspoken comments, but she hadn't asked or let her mom know she had been there to see her in such a broken moment.

It was the first time she had seen her mom as a person rather than just her mother. Her mom had feelings and fears, had made mistakes, had been through difficult things, wasn't happy about their current circumstances, and yet she loved her family and was trying to make the best of it.

Emily realized something else that day. Her mom often tried to guide her in her choices, she enforced rules and disciplined her when she needed it, she sometimes had to tell her 'no', and she asked for help around the house and taught her to be responsible; but when she made mistakes and did things she knew weren't right, her mom never brought it up later—like weeks or months after the fact. Once it was over, it was over. Her mom didn't harp on it like her grandmother was still doing about something that had happened a long time ago.

"I like this one," her mom said after looking through her notebook. Emily had finished her food and was taking a drink of water. "Do the stars mean you like it too?"

Emily went over to the bed and looked at the page for herself. She smiled because it was one of her favorites and one Tyler had liked also and written music for today.

"Yes," she replied. "Tyler played that one for the band."

"He likes this one?"

Emily knew why her mom was surprised. The song was totally about God. She almost hadn't read the words to him, but she had because of what he told her about praying for a dad and for his sister.

"It's his favorite," she said and explained why she thought so. "I think he knows God, Mom. Not in a church-way like I've learned about Him, but in a life-way. He's seen God provide in ways I've never had to ask for. And he's helping me to see Him in new ways."

"That's good to hear, honey," her mom said, giving her a hug. "I'll pray you both can grow closer to Jesus through your friendship. That's the way it was for your dad and me."

"Thanks, Mom. I never thought it would be like this."

"Like what?"

"That when my world fell apart, God would use it to bring everything together in a better way than I ever imagined."

~ CHAPTER TWENTY-THREE ~

On the morning of her skating competition, Brooke felt nervous as usual. She was getting more used to performing in front of a crowd, but she still had all the worries and doubts she'd had at her first competition. She wondered if she could really do this. She had images of tripping, falling, and not being able to do anything like she had practiced and perfected. She wanted to skate well for her coach, her family, her friends, the judges, and herself, but would she? That was the question of the day.

Once she got to the rink and had a chance to warm up on the ice, she felt better. Her wobbly legs became more confident and felt stronger as she got a feel for the ice and completed several of her jumps and spins. She'd had good practices this week and had every reason to believe she could do well today, but there was always that unknown factor of how she would do when all eyes were on her.

The thought made her feel sick to her stomach, so she tried not to think about it and focus on what she was doing, not what she might not do. She was glad her friends were coming today but felt nervous about skating in front of them. She knew Brianne, Emily, Allie, Austin, and Lindsay would still love her if she totally bombed, but she hoped she didn't. Brianne and Austin had seen her skate before and do well, so that took the pressure off somewhat, but she was doing a lot more difficult things today than the last time they had seen her compete.

Her greatest source of anxiety wasn't her friends, her family, or the judges, however. It came from her skating peers. The other girls in her division worried her more than anything. Their costumes seemed more beautiful and flashy than hers. Their skates looked newer. Their hair and makeup were perfect. And having them warm up around her, seeing them doing things she couldn't, made her question if she should be here and if she would come in dead last.

Off the ice while she was waiting for her turn to come, some of them were nice and talked to her, expressing their own anxiety and complimenting her costume and hairstyle. Others completely ignored her, and a few gave her looks of, 'Who are you, and what are you wearing?' She tried to ignore them as much as possible and remain in her own bubble, especially as her time to compete drew closer. She listened to music and found a quiet spot to lie down; and she prayed silently, asking Jesus to give her peace and calm her heart.

She had another chance to warm up when it was her group's turn to skate. It was only for a few minutes, but it calmed her. She didn't tire herself out because she was going first once the warm-up time was over, and she was glad. The less waiting, the better.

When her name was called, she received a smile from Elsa and skated out to the center of the rink. Getting into her opening pose, she waited for the music to begin, feeling her nerves escalate during those few seconds that seemed like an eternity, but once the music started, she went into motion, and she felt fully aware of what she was doing and numb to it at the same time. It was a weird sensation she always experienced but could never feel until it was happening.

She skated around the rink, performing one element after another, trying to remember all the little details and yet keep her concentration on the most difficult moves. After the first few were behind her, she relaxed more and tried to enjoy herself, but she wasn't able to relax fully until she finished. She knew she had done well in terms of completing everything and not making any major mistakes, but she didn't know how it looked to everyone until she got a loud ovation from the crowd. Skating off the ice and meeting her coach on the side, she knew she had done well by the look on Elsa's face. She was crying, and Brooke felt the tears come to her eyes as well.

"So beautiful," Elsa said. "Perfect, darling. Absolutely perfect!"

She hadn't looked in the direction of where her family and friends were sitting before her performance, but she turned and looked at them now, and they cheered as she waved and acknowledged their presence. While she waited for her scores to be posted, she caught her breath and felt incredibly happy. Even if the scores weren't great, she wouldn't care much at this point. She wanted to do well, but she also wanted to do her best, and she already knew she had done that.

Her scores were good though, higher than she had ever gotten before, and higher than she had realistically dreamed about. She knew the judges could be really picky, so their high scores told her she not only had a mistake-free performance but they were also satisfied with her technique and style—something she had a good foundation for and could only improve on from here.

The first person she hugged later, after her own family, was Brianne. "You were so awesome!" she said.

"Thanks," she replied. "And thanks for coming."

"I wouldn't have missed it," Brianne replied, and Brooke knew she meant that.

***

Sarah wasn't certain who was going to drive her to the bus station to pick up Ryan from his midmorning trip, or whom she would feel most comfortable having there, but when her brother offered to be the chauffeur, she was glad. Scott could tease her about it and she wouldn't mind, and she knew deep down he always supported her decisions.

He was curious on the drive there. He wanted to know what Ryan coming today meant exactly, and why she was choosing to allow it. She was honest and said she wasn't entirely certain on either count, but mostly she felt this was something she needed to do for herself and see what happened. Maybe this would change their relationship significantly, for good or bad, or maybe it wouldn't change much at all, but she wanted to find out, and she missed Ryan. That she knew, especially after waiting all week for today to get here.

Feeling nervous as they got out of the car, she was glad when Scott put his arm around her waist. He made her feel calmer, and his words were encouraging.

"No matter what happens today, sis, or any other time you spend with Ryan, I think you're brave for doing this."

"Really?" She laughed. "Why?"

"Because you're choosing a path of faith. Faith in your friendship with Ryan. Faith in him. Faith in yourself. And faith in Jesus to lead and carry you."

She hadn't thought about it like that, but she was taking this seriously. This was a big deal, for herself and for Ryan, and she wanted to treat it that way.

They didn't make it all the way to the door before she saw him. She hadn't seen Ryan since leaving Portland last year. And while she had always thought he was cute, she was reminded of that when she spotted him. He was taller and had a shorter hairstyle, but what really got her was his smile. It was the same as it had always been, but she had forgotten how it was when he looked right at her in person rather than seeing him in a photograph.

Scott remained behind as she went to meet him, and while Ryan's appearance brought the reality home he was actually here, his familiar greeting and closeness of a warm hug did something different to her heart. Any doubts she'd had about wanting to see him today melted away, and she knew he was hoping for that but cautious about expecting too much.

She didn't let go of his sweet hug too soon, wanting to convey her sincere excitement he was here, and that was easy to do. Ryan knew her well, and if she was having doubts about this, she wouldn't try to hide it, so an extended embrace from her could only mean one thing.

"It's good to see you, Sarah," he said, but she didn't let go.

"It's good to see you," she replied.

When she released her tight hold on his neck, she took another look at him and observed how he was looking at her. Neither view was surprising, and both were pleasant. He looked good, and he was happy to see her. She had been expecting him to be totally on board with being here, but he hadn't known exactly what to expect from her, and he was pleasantly surprised to get what he'd been hoping for.

"You've missed me," he said.

She was already smiling, and she laughed. "Yes, I have."

***

When Emily arrived home after Brooke's skating competition, she had just enough time to take a shower and get ready for going over to Tyler's house for dinner. She was happy Brooke had done so well and received first place, but now it was time for her big event of the day, and she felt more nervous about meeting Tyler's family than she expected.

She wasn't used to going to friends' homes where she didn't know the parents beforehand. Most of her friends she knew from church, dance class, or their homeschool association, so she had met at least one parent before going over to their house for dinner or a party.

Being at Tyler's was sure to be different than anything she had ever experienced, but she was comfortable enough spending time with Tyler to go through with their plans. Her dad drove her there at five-thirty, and he walked up to the door with her. He had met Tyler's mom and dad before when he had driven Tyler home, and when Tyler answered the door, Mr. Gunderson was there to greet them also, having a friendly exchange with her dad before turning his attention to her.

"You must be Emily," he said.

"I am," she replied, feeling a little awed by his dad's presence. He was younger-looking than she was expecting, and he had a very striking appearance—like an attractive movie star. Remembering this was the guy Tyler had prayed for to come into his mom's life, she suddenly had a new appreciation for God's ability to answer.

"Come on in," he said, stepping to the side and asking her dad if he wanted to come in for a few minutes.

"No, thank you," he replied. "I'll see you at eight-thirty, Emily."

"Okay," she replied, glancing over her shoulder before stepping inside and saying 'hi' to Tyler as his dad closed the door and then offered to take her coat. After she handed it to him, Mr. Gunderson stepped away, leaving them alone for a moment.

"Hey," Tyler said. "How was the skating competition?"

"Great! She won!"

"Really?"

"Yes. She was so good. I was so happy for her."

Tyler smiled and took her hand, leading the way to the kitchen. Emily saw two little girls' faces disappear just as she looked toward the archway they were approaching, followed by some giggling and an announcement to their mom that she was here.

She and Tyler entered the dining area first, and she could see the kitchen to the left with Tyler's two sisters in plain view along with Tyler's mom, who had a younger appearance than she had been expecting too, but it made sense.

"Emily," she said sweetly, coming over to meet her. "We're so glad you could come."

"Thank you," she replied. "I'm glad I could too."

~ CHAPTER TWENTY-FOUR ~

Emily hadn't known what to expect in coming to Tyler's house for dinner, but from the first moments when she arrived until they were sitting at the table eating delicious spaghetti and meatballs, green salad, bread, and steamed broccoli, she found it surprisingly delightful to be a guest in the unfamiliar setting. She had expected to feel comfortable with Tyler unless he acted differently than he had so far, but she hadn't expected to feel so comfortable getting to know his family.

His mom was really sweet, and his dad was very nice also. His sisters were silly, giggly girls who kept looking at her like she was a princess having dinner at their house, and Tyler was his usual self. He didn't seem nervous about having her here or like he had any reason to be worried about his parents meeting her. He let her speak for herself as they asked her lots of questions, and she felt comfortable answering them. While his sisters made her feel like a princess, Tyler and his parents treated her like an honored guest just for being herself.

She tried not to sound boastful about her various talents, and with as talented as Tyler was, she didn't have any room to brag around him, but he and his parents made her feel she had some special qualities.

They were also interested in her family and hearing about her years of being homeschooled and how she was feeling about the change to public school this fall.

Most of the questions she didn't find surprising, even if she hadn't specifically thought about what questions they might ask, but when Tyler's mom asked about the church she went to and how long her family had been attending, she was caught more off-guard. She answered honestly, and it wasn't a big deal, but because Tyler's family didn't attend church, she felt a little awkward sharing the information.

She had a fleeting thought about his mom saying, 'And why do you feel the need to drag my son there?', which would be completely out of character from how delighted she had seemed so far with her presence, but she imagined it anyway. In reality his dad spoke next on the subject, and his words were positive.

"When Tyler came home and asked if he could go every week with you, we knew this was serious."

He was teasing Tyler more than anything, and Tyler wasn't embarrassed. "He said, 'Wow she must be really pretty,'" Tyler added, "and I said, 'You've got that right.'"

From then on the conversation wasn't focused as much on her, but dinner continued in the pleasant manner it had started with. His mom brought out dessert not long after they were finished eating because Tatiana and Tasha were eager to have some. Emily accepted a piece of chocolate cake with raspberry sauce, but she didn't eat it right away because she felt full already. Tyler and his mom didn't either, and after his sisters were dismissed from the table, she and Tyler sat there talking to his mom and dad and enjoying their cake in a leisurely way.

Emily's only concern about tonight had been she and Tyler might be left with a lot of unsupervised time alone instead of being under the more watchful eyes of her parents, but they didn't have any time alone until after eight o'clock when she would be going home in twenty minutes. They had played a game at the table she'd never played before, but it was crazy and fun.

"Would you like a tour of the house?" Tyler asked as a way of excusing them. "We do have more than a kitchen and dining room."

She laughed. "Sure."

They went through the kitchen to where there was a large family room. His sisters were watching a movie, and it was obvious the room was used mainly for watching television and relaxing, but there was a deck off the large room he opened the sliding glass door to, and they stepped outside into the cool night air. It was still light out, and she could see the deck had a nice view of the horizon in the distance. She wasn't too surprised by that because it had been partially visible from the dining room windows, and houses in this area often had views of the valley.

From there they went down the outside stairs to a large outdoor entertainment area. There was another deck with an above-ground pool on the backside of it and a barbecue area with patio furniture and a hot tub.

"I like the outside of this house more than the inside," Tyler commented, reaching for her hand and turning to face her.

"It's nice," she replied. "You could have some cool parties next summer."

"Will you come?" he asked.

"Sure."

He smiled. "You don't think you'll be tired of me by then?"

"I hope not."

He laughed. "I hope not too."

"Your family is nice," she said.

"They like you."

"Yeah?"

"Oh, yeah. No doubt in my mind."

He continued with the tour, taking her in the basement doors that opened up to a large rec room where they had a pool table set up, but the rest of it was filled with boxes they were still unpacking. There was a bathroom, a small bedroom, and a storage area they passed as they went up the stairs and entered the front hall.

"My mom and dad's room is down there," he said pointing to a short hallway. "And there are three bedrooms upstairs."

Walking the opposite way, he took her into a living room with a sitting area in the front half by a large bay window. The back of the room was an office space with a computer and bookshelves. Along the wall between the main spaces was a piano, and it was beautiful.

She was drawn to it, and Tyler seemed to know she would be. He said it had been his grandparents' before they gave it to his mom as a housewarming gift when his parents bought their home in Astoria.

"Were you old enough to remember that?" she asked.

"Yes. My mom cried, but I didn't understand why or know that was a good thing until later."

She sat down on the squeaky wooden bench, and he joined her. "Play something," she said.

He started to play one of her songs, but she stopped him.

"Not that. Something you would have played two weeks ago."

He kept playing. "You don't like this?"

She smiled. "I love it, but I want to hear something you played before you knew me."

He segued into something more classical, but it wasn't a piece she specifically recognized.

"Haydn?" she guessed after a few moments.

"No, Gunderson."

"You wrote this?"

He smiled.

"Tyler! It's amazing! You're so gifted."

Emily heard another voice behind them. "I've been telling him that for three years," his mom said. "He wrote that for my birthday when he was eleven."

Emily turned and smiled at her. "Have you heard what he's written in the last week?"

"I hear him in here," she said.

"He told me you play too," Emily said.

"Yeah, Mom," Tyler said, removing his fingers from the keyboard and rising from the bench. "Come play something for us."

"I just play notes from a page," she laughed.

"And you play them well."

"I want to hear Emily play," she said.

Emily thought Tyler would insist his mom come play, but he took his mom's side and smiled.

"You heard the lady. Play us something, Emily."

"I don't have any music."

"And I don't believe that makes a difference for a second," he laughed.

She didn't take a lot of time to think about what to play. She had several favorites she'd memorized, but some were too serious and intense for a living room impromptu recital, so she chose one that was more flowing and wasn't terribly difficult.

"You have a beautiful touch, Emily," Mrs. Gunderson commented when she finished.

"Thank you," she replied, glancing at Tyler and seeing his silent agreement, but she wasn't thinking solely about herself. "It must be her turn now, huh?"

"Yeah, Mom. Your turn."

"Emily has to go in a few minutes," she said.

"Well, hurry up then."

Emily rose from the bench and laughed. Joining Tyler where he was standing, she watched as his mom gave in and stepped toward the piano. Emily thought Tyler might suggest something, but he remained silent and they both saw his dad enter the room. Mr. Gunderson didn't announce his presence and realized what they were doing without having to ask. He smiled as his wife took a seat and laughed nervously about being coerced into doing this.

Eventually she began to play, and Emily wasn't surprised by her proficiency. She had a beautiful touch too, and Emily knew she could listen to Tyler or his mom play for hours, but the doorbell ringing cut his mom short, and Emily supposed it was her mom or dad coming to pick her up.

Tyler's dad went to get the door. Emily decided to say something while it was just Tyler and his mom there, rather than waiting until she was leaving. Her parents had taught her to thank the parents of her friends who had her over to their house, and she always did, but usually it wasn't especially heartfelt, just something she did out of politeness. But tonight her words were sincere.

"Thank you for inviting me," she said to his mom first. "I had a really nice time."

"You're welcome," she replied. "I'm glad you were able to come."

"Me too. I can see where Tyler gets his love of music from, and his sweetness."

It was already obvious to Emily that Tyler's mom was proud of him, but she saw that pride increase as she smiled and glanced at him. He looked mildly embarrassed but knew his mom would be happy to hear how she saw him and how he treated her.

"He's turning out all right, I think," Mrs. Gunderson said. "And him choosing a friend like you, Emily, is evidence of that. You are welcome here anytime."

She saw both her mom and dad had come, and Mrs. Gunderson stepped over to be introduced to her mom whom she hadn't met yet. Emily took the opportunity to say something to Tyler before the adults turned their attention back to them.

"I had a great time. Thanks for inviting me."

"I'm glad tomorrow is Sunday and we get to do this again at your house."

"Me too," she replied.

~ CHAPTER TWENTY-FIVE ~

Sarah's day with Ryan consisted of lots of fun moments and laughter, and also serious talks. After returning to her house this morning, they'd had lunch together on the patio on the warm September day, and she told him all about her summer and how her first weeks of school had gone. He did the same and then suggested they go see a movie, so her mom drove them to the theater. Sarah said she would call when they needed to be picked up, but they decided to go shopping after the movie and then got dinner at the mall's food court where they talked for a long time about their spiritual lives, which Sarah didn't realize she needed to talk about until she was doing so.

Ryan was undergoing changes too, but he was steady in his faith, and she didn't have a lot of friends she could say that about. He was considering doing something next summer she was supportive of. He wanted to be involved in a local mission project that helped the homeless and low-income families. The youth group in Portland was already making plans for it and raising money, and she said she would give him some she currently had and as much as she could between now and then from her allowance and babysitting earnings.

She said it without much thought, but he reminded her that such a generous heart wasn't the norm among their peers. Even some of the kids in his youth group didn't want to participate because they had to raise their own money, rather than the church paying for everything they would need to help anyone.

She was still thinking about helping out at camp for a few weeks with Brianne, if the camp gave fifteen-year-olds that option next year. Her youth group did service projects during the summer and sent students on mission trips, but she had to be sixteen for that. Ryan reminded her summer was still a lot of months away so it was okay if she didn't know what she was doing, which she knew was true, but sometimes the future was more interesting than her current life.

Spending the day with Ryan changed that, and by the time they were back at her house and taking a walk around her neighborhood for their last hour together, she knew she wanted to have this stable connection to Ryan, even if their main communication would have to be from a distance.

"Are you glad I came today?" he asked.

He reached for her hand, and it was the first time he had showed her any physical affection all day. She knew he was looking for more than, 'Yeah, I had a nice time. Maybe we can do it again in six months.'

"I am very glad you came today," she assured him. "I need this a lot, Ryan. I need you in my life. God made that really clear to me last week when I wrote that letter, and today just confirms it for me."

He stopped walking and turned to face her. He had a look on his face she knew well, but it had been a long time since she had seen it. He had been shorter then, with longer hair, a scrawny build, and less self-confidence, although even at twelve he'd had more maturity than the average seventh-grade boy.

He was almost fifteen now. His birthday was a few weeks after hers in December, and he wasn't just cute and friendly like he'd been when she first met him. He was attractive to her. He was so kind and sincere. He had been so patient with her, had never done anything to try and make her jealous to get her back, and a much needed email from him had been enough to make her want time like this with him again.

"Can I ask you something?" she said.

"Sure. Anything."

"Anything, really?"

He smiled. "Yes."

She whispered her request. "Will you be my boyfriend?"

He laughed. "No way. I tried that once and ended up with a broken heart."

"Then why are you holding both of my hands?"

"Why are you whispering?"

"Because I'm nervous."

He moved his hands to her waist. "Why are you nervous?"

She smiled and played along. "No reason, I guess. Since you don't want me to be your girlfriend."

"I want that more than anything, Sarah."

She had said everything she needed to say today, and there wasn't a doubt in her mind she wanted Ryan to be a special part of her heart—like he had once been, only more so.

"Are you nervous about what I think you're nervous about?" he asked with an adorable expression on his face.

"Yes," she replied.

"Are you sure? I didn't come here today expecting anything."

"I know you didn't. And if you don't want to, it's fine. But if you do, I'm ready. I'm ready to do this, Ryan. All of it."

He gave the open invitation to kiss her serious consideration, she could tell, but she knew almost immediately he wasn't going to. Not today, but maybe sometime soon.

"That's tempting, Sarah," he sighed. "But I think we should wait. If we both really want this, we can take that step when we know the time is right, but if I kiss you right now, we can't take it back. It will forever change both of us, and I don't want to do that until I know for sure that will be a good thing."

She appreciated his wisdom and restraint, and it only reminded her of what a good friend he had always been to her. "Will you come see me again soon?"

"Yes," he replied.

She said good-bye to him thirty minutes later in front of the bus station, but she knew he would be back, and in a way she was glad they were separated by distance right now. She knew she would miss him during the week and on the weekends he couldn't be here, but she also knew their times together would be that much sweeter because of it.

Three weeks passed before she saw him again, but she went to Portland to see him there. And not just him, but Brianne, Austin, Brooke, Marissa, Emily, Tyler, Michael, and David too. Brianne had arranged for David to spend Columbus Day Weekend in Clatskanie. He was staying at Austin's house, and on Saturday evening they all went to a concert together in Portland. Her brother drove her up in the morning to see Ryan, and they had the whole day together before meeting the others at the concert and then she went home with Brianne that night to spend Sunday and Monday with her.

From her perspective it was a fun weekend, but Brianne was a little stressed with having David there. She was happy about him coming, going to the concert, and the band working on his music, but she was stressed about how to act around him. Sarah understood her anxiety and knew it came mainly from her uncertainty about how she felt about him, and how that fit into her friendship with Austin.

"You might be nervous and unsure on the inside, Brianne," she said to her on Monday morning before they were going to be meeting David and the band at the church for one last jam session. "But it doesn't show. You're just being yourself, and I don't think Austin or David are expecting anything from you that you're not living up to."

"I'm trying to let it be about the music."

"I think it is. For now, anyway. David and Austin might have hopes about the future, but they're not trying to go there yet, at least not that I can see."

"I know. It's weird. Whenever I'm around David, he acts like I'm just another girl, but then when he writes to me, he says all this stuff about liking me."

Sarah smiled. She didn't know if she should tell Brianne her thoughts on that, but Brianne insisted once she could see she had something to say.

"I know you didn't notice David when we were at camp, and you were surprised when he asked for your address, but that's only because he's quiet. He may not have talked to you until the last day, but you're the only girl he talks to."

"He's been talking to Emily."

"About music, yes, but not anything else."

Austin's dad drove up then and they got into the truck to ride to the church. David was sitting in the front, and she and Brianne got into the back with Austin, but once they were at the church, Sarah saw more of the same in the interaction between Brianne and David.

It wasn't like the casual and easy friendship she had with Austin, but it wasn't like watching two people who didn't know how to talk to each other either. It was somewhere in between that. It reminded her of the way she and Ryan had always been right from the start. The difference was that while she had been able to see Ryan every day at school when they were first getting to know each other, Brianne and David only had a few hours while he was here visiting and while all of her friends, including Austin, were around.

Sarah would want to be a fly on the wall when, if ever, they had times when it was just the two of them. But she couldn't imagine when that might happen unless Brianne deliberately allowed it.

Austin's dad took David and herself back to Portland that afternoon. David was catching the train, and Scott was meeting them there to drive her back to Eugene. Austin and Brianne went along too. This time Austin rode up front, and she and Brianne rode in the back with David.

Scott called her when they were getting close to Portland. He thought they were going to be there by five, but they were actually shooting for five-thirty. She knew they would probably be there by five-fifteen unless the traffic got bad between here and the train station. He said it wasn't a big deal, he was just wondering where they were. After she hung up, she could hear David was saying something to Brianne, but she couldn't hear his every word. She caught something about his youth group and a conference they were going to over Winter Break, and then the next words she heard clearly.

"You can think about it and let me know. When I heard we were going to be near Bellingham, I thought you might be up there then too."

Sarah knew Brianne often went to Bellingham for Christmas with her family to visit her grandparents and assumed she must have mentioned that to David at some point. She didn't have to wait long to hear Brianne respond.

"Yeah, I probably will be. That would be nice."

~ CHAPTER TWENTY-SIX ~

Brianne tried to get her homework done on the drive back to Clatskanie, but she had a difficult time concentrating. Austin was working on his math but kept interrupting her for help, and the reading she had to do for literature was boring and tedious. The writing was difficult to follow, the characters complicated and confusing, and the storyline slow.

When Austin moved over to take the seat beside her instead of the one by the door, she was in the middle of a paragraph, but she had no idea what was going on. She couldn't remember who Aunt Libby was and why she would be showing up at the protagonist's home and what significance that had. A few minutes ago she had been annoyed by Austin's interruptions, but now she welcomed it. Her lack of concentration didn't have anything to do with him, but she did wonder why he was invading her space.

"You're finished?" she asked.

"No, I need a break. Want some m&m's?"

He was opening the yellow bag, and she smiled. She could use some chocolate, and his company wasn't anything to turn down either. Holding out her hand, she waited for him to dump the colored candy into her palm, and he wasn't stingy with his sharing, giving her at least half the bag before stopping to keep the rest for himself.

She allowed her book to close without bothering to put in a bookmark. She needed one hand to hold the m&m's and the other to pop the first one into her mouth. The book was just a nuisance getting in the way.

She savored the flavor of the chocolate and the crunchy peanut as Austin ate one of his. She let out a sigh, and he stated the obvious.

"Not enjoying the book?"

"It's horrible. I have no idea what's going on, and I couldn't care less. What chapter are you on?"

"I only read the first chapter."

"Austin! Aren't you supposed to read through Chapter Four by tomorrow too?"

"Yes, but David told me what it's about and how it ends and all the major stuff I need to know. He had to read it last year."

"Well, tell me!"

He told her what he knew, and it was helpful, but she didn't know if it was enough to get her through the quiz they would have tomorrow. Austin's teacher didn't give weekly quizzes on the reading, just expected them to have it finished by the end of the reading schedule and then write an essay on the topic of their choice. Mrs. Kirk wasn't so easy-going about required ninth-grade reading material, so Brianne knew she would still have to read it for herself, but hopefully hearing the synopsis would help.

"Why didn't you have David help you with your math?" she teased him.

"Because I have you for that," he replied.

She smiled and realized she felt relaxed for the first time in three days. She liked having David and Sarah here, and it had been a good weekend with everyone, but she'd felt stressed much of the time. She tried not to be, but her anxiety had never gone away. David was nice, and she liked him, and he fit in well with her friends, but she wasn't completely comfortable around him yet. She didn't know him well enough or know what to expect from him.

But Austin was a different story. Sometimes she felt like she knew him better than she knew herself. And even when he surprised her, it was a good surprise. Nothing about this weekend had surprised her too much, and she didn't think it could have gone any better, but she knew he was largely responsible for that.

"What else did you and David talk about when I wasn't around?" she inquired.

"Music mostly, and you."

"Me?"

"He likes you," Austin said matter-of-factly. "A lot."

"He said that?"

"He didn't have to."

"How do you know?"

"Guys don't talk about girls the way David talks about you unless they do."

"What did he say?"

"He thinks you're more real and mature than most of the girls in his youth group, even the older ones. And he emphasized to me several times he wants you to sing his songs, not Emily or Marissa. He thinks they sing fine, but these songs were written for you to sing."

She often tried to defer the lead vocals to someone else and had mostly succeeded. "Why didn't he tell me that?"

"I think he wanted to but didn't know how when everyone was together. He shared his thoughts more freely when it was just me and him. He probably would have with you if he'd had that chance, but he didn't."

She thought about how he had only spoken to her in a more personal and private way on the drive this afternoon when Sarah was talking on her phone. And she told Austin what he'd said, knowing it was going to come out eventually and wanting his honest opinion on the matter.

"He wants to come back next month. Like maybe the weekend before Thanksgiving."

"I know. He asked me if that would be all right."

She wasn't surprised. "Did he tell you he's going to be in Bellingham for Christmas Break too?"

"No," Austin smiled. "He didn't tell me that."

She laughed. Austin had been good about all of this, but she could see that bit of news pushing him to the edge. "I would probably only see him for a couple of hours one afternoon."

"This is a nightmare," he said, leaning his head back against the seat and closing his eyes. "Either you have to stop being so adorable, or I have to stop being nice to these guys."

"Did you enjoy this weekend at all? Or was it stressful for you too?" she asked him seriously. Yesterday was his birthday, and they'd had a party for him last night after spending the afternoon working on music with the band, but she felt worried about it being the same weekend David had come for a visit.

He opened his eyes. "It was all right. Why were you stressed?" he asked, seeming surprised and confirming Sarah's words about her not showing it.

"It was fine, but I never knew what to expect. Before this weekend I'd only talked to David for thirty seconds, and I didn't know he liked me then."

"He's a good guy, Brianne. You know why I think he wanted to come, beside to see you again?"

"To work on music?"

"Yes, but more than that, he's in need of good friendships. Something I noticed about him at camp was he spent a lot of time alone. I didn't even know there were other guys from his youth group there that week until Thursday, but after seeing the way they acted, I wasn't surprised."

"How did they act?"

"Like high school guys—jocks, trying to impress the girls, arrogant, not really into God—like some of the guys we have. I don't think he mentioned anyone from his church all weekend. He has more friends at school than he has there."

Hearing that changed Brianne's perspective on having David as a friend. Maybe at some point in the future she would have a romantic relationship with him, but for now he needed her to be his friend, like she needed Austin and Austin needed her. And she knew from having a strong friendship with Sarah that being a friend from a distance was possible. It just took extra effort to maintain.

When she got home, she finished up her homework and then wrote David a letter, letting him know she had enjoyed having him here and he was welcome to come again next month. She also gave him her email address and said he could write to her that way anytime, rather than waiting until he had more lyrics to send.

I'm choosing to only have guys as friends right now, as you know, but I'm serious about those friendships, and I don't want you to think I'm being nice to you but secretly wish you would leave me alone. Anything you feel comfortable sharing with me, I want you to share it. Anything you want to ask me, just ask, and I'll always be honest with you about how I feel.

Something that really stood out to me over the weekend is how genuinely nice you are and how authentic you are about your faith. I don't see both of those qualities in people our age very often, but when I do, I notice, and I need friends like that. I crave real friendships based on honesty, trust, caring, and Jesus, and something tells me you do too. I am honored to be your friend.

Sincerely,
Brianne

I love to hear from my readers

Write me at:

living_loved@yahoo.com

Additional Titles in the
True Friendship Series:

Just Smile

Rescue Me

Just Wait

Made in the USA
Middletown, DE
09 February 2017